D0289292

Trip of a Lifetime

Trip of a Lifetime

The Adventures of Dillon and Kyle

By
Dr. Dennis S. Atkinson

Illustrated by
Ray Hartland
&
Dennis Atkinson

Post Office Box 1099 • Murfreesboro, Tennessee 37133

All Scripture quotations are from
the King James Bible

The greatest way to learn about children is by interacting with them.

To

My greatest teachers, my own three children—Emilee, Julianna and Peter:

You gave me a gift of love for every boy and girl, for in each one I see a little bit of you. I learned why God adores little children and why He loves to be called "Abba, Father."

You were my greatest fans, even when I failed. You laughed when I told "unfunny" jokes, clapped when I was a flop and made me feel like I was a success when I was still learning the fine art of children's ministry.

This story is for you just as much as it is for all boys and girls around the world. We have had a "trip of a lifetime," and I wouldn't want to have "sailed" with anyone but you!

Contents

Acknowledgments

Special thanks to...

My wife, Pat, and my daughter Emilee for their many hours of editing and proofreading the manuscripts.

My retired sailor friends, Rev. Lawrence Shillingburg (QM/USN) and Mr. Bill Norman (USCG), who assisted me in some sound nautical information.

Ray Hartland, a gifted artist and faithful Christian who joined me in this project.

Dover Publications for the charts and maritime information gathered from George Biddlecombe.

The hundreds of boys and girls at Church of the Open Door and Carroll Christian Schools, Westminster, Maryland who insisted on book Number Two. Thank you for your support.

Chapter 1
The Trip of a Lifetime

"Ring-ring, ring-ring."

Dillon heard the telephone ringing in his bedroom. It was Tuesday afternoon, and he had some homework to do. A test, some arithmetic problems and a chapter to read for science were all he could do for the evening. Interruptions wouldn't help him get it all done. Slowly he walked over to the phone, hoping that someone else would pick it up.

"Hello, Holecheck resid—" he began, but before he could get it all out, he was interrupted by a familiar voice.

"Dillon, is that you?"

"Sure it's me. Who did you think it was, Abraham Lincoln?"

"Did you check your mailbox yet?" Kyle asked anxiously.

"No, I didn't. Why do you ask?"

"I got mine!" Kyle shouted as he bubbled with unusual excitement.

A shocked look came over Dillon's face as he deliberately said, "You mean you got—"

Before he could finish that sentence, Kyle squealed on the other end of the phone, "Yes, I got my acceptance letter to travel!"

"Hold on," Dillon commanded as he dropped the telephone, abandoning it to dangle on the side of the wall.

He ran down the stairs to the living room and rushed out the door, sending the screen door into a slam against the side of the house. He dashed to the mailbox, pulled down on the door and grabbed the pile of mail.

He began to sort through the mail until he found a large, light-blue envelope with his name on it. The letter displayed a picture of a three-masted ship, and below the picture words in bold letters jumped out at him: **URGENT! OPEN IMMEDIATELY!**

Dillon tore it open and read the letter inside.

"Yippee!" he screamed. He stuffed the other mail back in the mailbox without closing the door and bounced down the sidewalk toward Kyle's house. In all his excitement, Dillon forgot that Kyle was on the phone waiting for him. "All right!" he shouted as he ran. Every few houses he would jump in the air while he was running, wave the letter and yell, "Yippee!"

Dillon didn't stop until he arrived at Kyle's house. He ran up to the unlocked front door and went right in. They were such good friends that Kyle's parents didn't mind his not knocking.

Kyle was still sitting at the kitchen table with the phone to his ear. Facing the other direction, he didn't hear or see Dillon come in.

"Dillon, are you there? Dillon...Dillon...!" Kyle was shouting into the phone, hoping to get Dillon's attention.

"Yes, I'm here!" answered Dillon.

Kyle didn't know Dillon was in the room as he continued to speak into the mouthpiece. "Well, did you get your letter yet?"

Dillon tapped Kyle on the shoulder and said, "I'm right here, Silly." He scared Kyle so much that he jumped off his chair.

Dillon continued talking, unaware that he

had just scared his friend half to death. "And I got mine!" he shouted in delight. The boys went hopping outside as Dillon waved his letter high in the air. "It says we board the ship in three weeks."

You see, the two had read about an opportunity for young boys to sail on an old tall ship like the ones sailors and pirates used to sail before engines were invented to move the ships. It was a full-rigged ship, which means three masts of sails with a set of jib sails and a spanker in the back. This powered the ship by means of the wind.

The name of the beautiful ship was the USS *SkipJack*.

The experience aboard the ship would teach them not only what it was like aboard one of those ships but also how to sail and work the rigging. Their parents were told that it would teach them teamwork and character, but the boys didn't care about that stuff. Dillon and Kyle just wanted to take a sailing adventure, a trip of a lifetime.

The very thought of hoisting the sails, steering the ship, towing lines, pulling up the anchor and cutting through the ocean waves sent goose bumps of excitement up and down their backs.

During the trip, they would be part of a crew of twenty recruits, with fifteen experienced sailors to train them. Dillon and Kyle had been praying and hoping for two months that they would be accepted as part of that twenty. The boys had submitted their applications and were waiting for a reply. Now they had their passage confirmation, which promised they were to become crew members and real, live sailors would teach them the art of sailing.

The confirmation letter gave them instructions on where to go, what to do and what to bring. It also instructed them to call the captain of the USS *SkipJack* if they had a change of heart and no longer wanted to go.

If they accepted the invitation, the letter said, they would receive crew member uniforms in the mail within two weeks. It included shirts, bell-bottom pants, a necktie and special shoes to wear aboard the ship. They were to wear the uniforms when they reported for duty on June 21. The letter also gave them a list of items they would need for the eight-week experience.

"Didn't José send in an application too?" asked Dillon.

"He sure did. Let's give him a call. He probably got his letter too."

Kyle went to the phone and dialed the number.

"Hello?"

"Hey, José, this is Kyle."

"Hey, Kyle, what's up?"

"I was calling to see if you got an acceptance letter to sail on board the USS *SkipJack* in June."

"Yeah, I got it, but I'm not going," said José gruffly. "I'm not interested in all that character-building stuff. I'll stay around here and have some fun this summer."

Kyle couldn't believe his ears. "You're kidding, aren't you? I mean, this is the chance of a lifetime."

"Maybe to you it is, but not to me. I'm

going to go swimming and sleep out in my tent. I called 'em and told 'em I wasn't coming. You guys should do the same. We could have a great time if you stuck around. I'd see to it! Well, anyway, let me know. I've gotta go. Bye."

Kyle stared blankly at the phone as he slowly hung up.

"Well, what did he say?"

"He's not going. He got an invitation and everything, but he said it would be dumb," Kyle replied, as Dillon looked at him in disbelief.

"Whatever," said Dillon, as he shrugged his shoulders. "It's his loss, not ours. He's the one who will miss out on the trip."

The two weeks went quickly by. Just as promised, the uniforms arrived by special delivery. Kyle took his to Dillon's house, where they tried them on. Wow, did they ever look sharp!

They chuckled with anticipation as they talked about the great time they were going to have. Their imaginations began to soar with possibilities.

"I can see us working on the ship now," said Kyle, "climbing the sails high above the deck, looking for pirates from the crow's house and shooting the cannons."

"I think the word is crow's *nest,* and I doubt that there are any pirates around anymore. I also doubt they are going to let us shoot cannons at anyone." Dillon laughed thinking about this.

"I guess you're right. We'll probably be mopping decks and cooking food for the captain. But I don't care. Look how great we look in these uniforms," he said as he looked admiringly in the mirror.

Soon school was out, and they began to pack and prepare for the trip.

Before we go any further, let me remind you what the Bible says about another "trip of a lifetime." We call it Heaven. We can notice several similarities between our getting to go to Heaven and the boys' going on a sea adventure.

First, they were given an invitation to sail aboard the USS *SkipJack*. We also are given an invitation by God to go to Heaven. It says in John 3:16:

"For God so loved the world, that he gave his only begotten Son, that whosoever believeth in him should not perish, but have everlasting life."

In other words, God has given us an opportunity to accept the gift of eternal life with Him. This is our invitation to believe on Jesus to save us from our sin and take us to Heaven.

Second, the boys were given clean, white uniforms. The boy or girl who receives Jesus as his or her Saviour also receives a uniform from God called "the robe of righteousness."

Now, don't get me wrong. This uniform is not one we wear on earth that can be seen. It's a uniform only God can see. The Bible talks about it in Isaiah 61:10:

"I will greatly rejoice in the LORD, my soul shall be joyful in my God; for he hath clothed me with the garments of salvation, he hath covered me with the robe of right-eousness, as a bridegroom decketh himself

19

with ornaments, and as a bride adorneth herself with her jewels."

Notice, our robe is a garment "of salvation" and "of righteousness." That new uniform is spotless. We can only enter Heaven if God gives us this "robe of righteousness." This invisible robe is put on us when we receive Jesus as our Saviour.

Third, the boys received an absolutely awesome gift. In fact, they would not know how wonderful it was until it was over. The Bible tells us that we receive an indescribable gift from God when we trust Christ as our Saviour. Heaven is such a wonderful place—too wonderful to describe. First Corinthians 2:9 says:

"But as it is written, Eye hath not seen, nor ear heard, neither have entered into the heart of man, the things which God hath prepared for them that love him."

Boys and girls, there are so many wonderful things about God and His Heaven that only time and sight can explain. One day those who have trusted Christ as Saviour will appreciate receiving a "trip of a lifetime."

Have you accepted God's invitation of eternal life? If you haven't, then bow your head now and ask God to save you from your sin. Ask Jesus to make you one of His children now.

The morning had come when Dillon and Kyle were to meet the USS *SkipJack* at the harbor in Annapolis, Maryland. The sun was shining brightly as Dillon and his parents made their way to Kyle's house, where they would pick up him and his parents for the trip to the harbor. The boys piled their belongings into the minivan. Everything imaginable was packed and placed in "gunnies," or linen bags, that had a drawstring at the top and were used by sailors to stow their gear.

The boys stood proudly in their new uniforms, which bore an insignia of the USS *SkipJack* on the upper right shoulder. Name badges were sewn above their chest pockets, just like the badges of real sailors. They couldn't be more excited than they were at that moment.

The three-hour ride to Annapolis was filled with instructions from Kyle's parents, lessons on the history of Annapolis, home of the United States Naval Academy, and just plain chatter from the boys.

On the trip, the boys noticed sea gulls soaring in the sky above them. The rolling hills of Maryland soon began to flatten out as they approached the shores of Chesapeake Bay, a body of water which flows quietly into the Atlantic Ocean. Many battles took place in those waters. Not too far from Annapolis stood Fort McHenry, the inspiration for Francis Scott Key's anthem, "The Star-Spangled Banner."

"Boy, I can smell the salty air from the bay. Can you?" Dillon asked, as he poked Kyle in the side with his elbow.

"Me too," replied Kyle.

It was then that the car traveled over a bridge rising high above the water. "What's the name of this river?" Kyle asked his dad as he pushed his head against the glass of the rear side door.

"That's not a river, Kyle. It is an inlet that

gets its water from the harbor. In another fifteen minutes or so, we'll be at our destination."

Chapter 2
Learning the Ropes

"Oh, look!" Dillon excitedly blurted out. "I can see some of the ships now!"

As the van approached the harbor parking lot, they could see many beautiful yachts anchored to the docks of the marina. The boats were all different sizes. They appeared to be a bright, shiny white, with navy blue trim and glistening chrome that mirrored the images of the harbor.

As the minivan pulled to a stop in the parking lot overlooking the rippling, bluish-green water, the boys popped open the van doors and jumped out, their eyes scanning the water. The harbor was alive with the

sounds of sea gulls screeching, a tug boat chugging up the harbor with a "blub-blub," ships' owners talking to one another, and men giving orders to the shipmates. Activity accompanied the marine sounds, which filled the air like music. It was truly the most beautiful sight the boys had ever seen.

But the most beautiful sight of all was

the USS *SkipJack* resting in the deep water out in the middle of the harbor. Big chains running through the hawsepipe in the bow of the ship poked into the water to anchor it securely. Three large masts rose up from the decks, supporting the sails that were neatly folded in rolls along the yardarms. The old ship floated in the water as proudly as any ship could.

"Well, boys, you'd better get your gear and carry it over to where the others are standing," Kyle's father suggested.

"Okay, Dad," Kyle answered.

The boys were so excited they could hardly talk. They grabbed their bags and made their way over to join the other boys, who seemed just as nervous and excited as Dillon and Kyle.

"Turn around and smile," said Dillon's mother as she held up a camera ready to take the shot. The boys turned around with big smiles, the picturesque harbor behind them.

"Got ya," she said. "Now don't forget to be good and to brush your teeth."

"We won't forget, Mom," Dillon replied. "Don't worry about us; we'll be just fine. After all, we are eleven years old."

The boys' parents got the boys checked in properly, prayed with them, said their good-byes and were soon driving out of sight.

Kyle was still waving when he heard a stern, commanding voice. "Dillon! Kyle!" The two turned to see one of the sailors addressing them. "You boots stand over to the starboard with the others! Take your gunnysacks and be quick about it, or you'll be sailing two fathoms below the mud hook!"

"Aye, aye, Sir," they answered in unison. They weren't sure if they were to say, "Yes, Sir," or "Aye, aye, Sir," but they figured they did the right thing when the sailor turned away from them and gave his attention to another recruit.

They found out later that "boot" was another term for a new recruit in the Navy. "I hope I can figure out what these crew members are talking about," said Kyle.

"Me too. I don't want to end up in Davy Jones' locker," answered Dillon.

"Davy Jones' locker?" Kyle questioned, a puzzled look on his face. "Who's Davy Jones, and why would we end up in his locker?"

"That's more Navy talk for the bottom of the sea," Dillon said, smiling. "I read that in a book last year. It's definitely not a place you wanna be."

As the boots were standing in single file along the dock, a shrill whistle, the boatswain's pipe, was blown: "EE-AH!" A slender sailor approached the boots and

then walked slowly past each, eyeing him up and down. "Ahoy there, mates. I'm Mr. Jars, the second mate of the *SkipJack*," he said with a friendly but serious tone. "I'm here to escort you to the ship. If any of you want to turn back, now is your chance. I'll not lie to you. It will be hard work, and no one will be given special treatment. But I will tell you this: Once you begin ta learn the ways of the sea and how ta handle the ship, you'll find it to be a rewardin' experience. You'll be sad to leave it all."

Mr. Jars turned and walked up the line of recruits once again. "If you're ready for such an adventure, then pick up your gunnies and board the whaleboats."

The boys boarded the small boats and motored out toward the *SkipJack*. The closer they got to the ship, the larger it appeared. They didn't realize how large it was until they saw it up close.

None of the boots talked much on the short trip. They were too nervous and a little frightened by what Mr. Jars had said.

"Part of me wants to go on this adventure, and part of me wants to turn back," Kyle whispered in Dillon's ear.

"I know what you mean," Dillon said with an unusually short response as he sat on the hard, wooden seat.

The boat soon pulled alongside the *SkipJack* where a ladder made of rope was thrown over the side. The sailor operating the boat pointed toward the ladder and commanded, "That's Jacob's ladder. Get your gear and make your way up to the *angels* above. And be quick about it, ye landlubbers! I ain't got all day!"

The boys didn't argue. Their feet tangled with the rope, and their gunnysacks fought against them as they climbed up the side of the ship. The seamen laughed at the whole sight and heckled them from above, even though they did try to help them up.

The recruits made their way on board ship. Once aboard, they formed a straight line amidships (the middle of the ship) while facing the forecastle (front) of the ship.

An older man with a white beard and dressed in a pressed blue uniform studied the boys as they stood quietly. They soon learned this was the captain. His face was tanned and hardened by the sun and many years at sea. Although his face was stern, you could see a twinkle of kindness in his eyes and a love for what he was doing.

When the last boy boarded, the bosun, a junior officer responsible for maintenance on deck, blew the boatswain's pipe: "EE-AH-EH." When the sound echoed across the deck, every sailor stood at attention and faced the captain. The recruits took the cue from them and also stood at attention.

The captain faced the new crew members and addressed them.

"Good afternoon. I'm Captain Blair. I welcome you aboard the USS *SkipJack*. You will find this an experience you will never want to forget. For years to come, you will remember the lessons you have learned here.

"The lives of everyone on board are your responsibility. If you fail to perform your duty to its fullest, you will be putting your crew mates in jeopardy. It is, therefore, necessary that you be on time, work hard, learn every aspect of the ship, obey every order without complaint and take seriously the tasks assigned to you.

"If you do this well, then you will earn the respect due a sailor and a special patch to add to your uniform at the completion of your journey. It is a privilege awarded to the few who complete their tour with honor. I trust that you will strive to be one of those few.

"Your training will be under the care of my first mate, Mr. Riggs," he said, as he nodded in the direction of a sailor who looked hard and serious. "I would advise you to listen to him, for he knows his business well, having been a sailor for nearly thirty years. If you obey him, he will be your friend; if you are slothful, he will be your foe."

Kyle gave a big gulp. "I think I believe him," he whispered to Dillon.

Then the captain looked over to Mr. Riggs and directed, "Mr. Riggs, they are yours to command." With that, the captain turned and walked to the side of the ship and peered over the railing.

The recruits were escorted to their quarters below ship, and the other sailors helped them settle in and acquainted them with the layout of the ship.

The next two weeks were filled with instructions on how the ship operated, the name of each part and how to hoist the sails. There were practice drills and instructions on how to tie knots, coil the lines and maintain the tackling.

"The tackling of a ship is anything aboard that helps sail the *SkipJack*," Mr. Riggs taught. "It includes ropes or lines, pulleys, chains, blocks and rigging. It is important to take good care of them."

"I didn't know that being a sailor was such

hard work!" Dillon exclaimed to Kyle one night while they were resting. "I think I've learned more in these past two weeks than in my whole life!"

"Yeah, there sure are a lot of things to memorize and do. I've learned one thing though."

"What's that?"

"That a ship can't run itself. It needs a crew who can operate the rigging. In fact, the rigging is actually what makes the ship operate. I thought all you needed was a rudder to steer it, but the rigging and the crew are the heartbeat of the ship that propels and steers it."

★★★

The boys found out this important lesson about sailing: The lines, sails, pulleys, chains, masts and the rest of the rigging are essential parts of sailing a ship. With those tools, they can sail with or even against the wind by what is called "tacking."

As Christians, we too are like the rigging of a ship. "How's that?" you ask. Well, read

Romans 6:12-14 to find out:

"Let not sin therefore reign in your mortal body, that ye should obey it in the lusts thereof.

"Neither yield ye your members as instruments of unrighteousness unto sin: but yield yourselves unto God, as those that are alive from the dead, and your members as instruments of righteousness unto God.

"For sin shall not have dominion over you: for ye are not under the law, but under grace."

The word "instruments" was used in the apostle Paul's day as either the weapons of an army soldier or the rigging of a masted ship. Paul said that we could yield our members (or our body parts) as instruments of either righteousness or unrighteousness. You can use your body and mind for good or evil.

Imagine for a moment that you are a ship just like the *SkipJack*. On board you have the rigging of arms, legs, mouth, ears and a mind. What type of ship you want to be is up to you. You can be a merchant ship carrying cargo from one place to another, or a pirate ship stealing from others. You can be either a ship of righteousness (one that does right) or a ship of unrighteousness (one that does wrong).

Notice in verse 12 the word "let," which means "to allow." We have a choice: yielding either to God or to Satan. The Bible says that we Christians should yield our lives to the Captain of our souls, the Lord Jesus. We should let Him control our "instruments" to do good and right.

Our Captain is wise and concerned about the crew. He knows the waters and can guide us safely through life. It would be wise for us to trust Him.

Dillon and Kyle realized that the sailors aboard the *SkipJack* had to know their ship well. They knew every line, every part, every purpose of the rigging so that when it was needed they could guide the ship and obey the commands given.

We must also learn about life from the Bible. If we learn it well, we will be able to maneuver ourselves through the waters of life. Sometimes those waters can be dangerous and rough. If a crew is careless, the ship could be lost.

Don't be careless about your life. Learn how to sail safely and happily by learning the Word of God and following your Captain, Jesus.

As I said, the first two weeks were days of getting acquainted with the workings of the ship. There were parts the boys liked and parts they didn't like. Dillon and Kyle soon found why sailors wore bell-bottom pants. It made the pant legs easier to roll up into shorts when they swabbed the decks, a duty the sailors didn't enjoy very much.

Mr. Riggs was pretty particular about having a clean ship, and that required mopping every corner of it. If it wasn't cleaned properly, they had to do it over. They soon learned to do it right the first time.

However, not everything on the ship was hard work. Some things they did enjoy, as you will soon see.

Chapter 3
Cookie and Milk

One of the first things the boys had learned aboard ship was how to tell time. They didn't use wrist watches and clocks on the ship; instead, bells were sounded.

Dillon first noticed the shiny, brass bells when he stood at attention while waiting to meet Captain Blair. There were two bells aboard the ship, one larger than the other. The bells hung on a harp-shaped frame; the larger bell was at amidships, and the smaller one was attached to the wheel box.

The wheel box was like the steering wheel and was operated by the helmsman. It was the helmsman's job to be aware of the time by keeping the only clock on board ship. He would then ring the smaller bell by pulling on a lanyard made of white cotton cord. The lanyard, attached to a clapper, made a sharp strike against the side of the bell.

Mr. Jars, the second mate, explained to the new recruits how the bell system worked.

"The hours at sea are not referred to as 'o'clock' but as bell tones. On the half hour the bell sounds out an odd number of tones, and every hour the bell rings an even number of tones. For example," he explained, "one

ring is sounded for 12:30, and two rings, for one o'clock. It continues that way for a four-hour time period. When it is four o'clock, eight bells are sounded, and then it cycles all over again."

Mr. Jars then explained how days were divided into "watches." The men aboard the ship took turns keeping an eye out and watching for danger, hence the name "watches."

"There are seven watches, and each of you will take your turn. Each watch is four hours long except for the 'dog watches,' which are two hours each."

"Boy, I hope I can remember all these watches," whispered Dillon, exasperated from it all. "There's the dog watch, the anchor watch, the port watch, the light watch, the starboard watch, here a watch, there a watch, everywhere a watch watch!"

"The only watch I care about is Cookie's watch," answered Kyle.

The ship's cook's name was Jim Cook, and the crew had nicknamed him "Cookie." Cookie was the only sailor on board who didn't have to maintain watch. His whole job was cooking three meals daily for the crew.

"I think I like mealtime as much as anything," said Kyle.

"Me too," replied Dillon.

After Mr. Jars had finished explaining how the watches and bells worked, he dismissed them. Two minutes hadn't passed before the helmsman rang eight bells, which meant it was four o'clock in the afternoon. Then the larger bell was answered with eight bells: "Ding-ding, ding-ding, ding-ding, ding-ding."

"Sweet!" cried out Dillon. "It's dinnertime!"

Mr. Jars dismissed the crew. They hurried into the ship's kitchen, called the galley.

"What's for supper, Cookie?" asked Kyle.

"We're having dolphin casserole."

The first time the boys heard him mention dolphin casserole, they were a little shocked. After all, who would want to eat a dolphin for supper? Fortunately, it was only a name Cookie had made up for his famous hamburger casserole meal. It was made to taste like a hamburger. On the side, he prepared vegetables, fresh fruit and homemade apple pie. They could smell the aroma on board the ship all day long.

"I can hardly wait to sink my teeth into that pie," said Dillon, his mouth watering in delight.

"Before we eat our meal, I need to ask you a question," Cookie stated. "I've noticed some of my food disappearing lately. In fact, I've found traces of crumbs on the galley floor, crumbs that I didn't put there."

"Well, it wasn't me," quickly responded Milk.

Milk's real name was Tim. He had jet-black hair and was so fair skinned that one crew member said his skin was as white as milk. So they began to call him "Milk." Dillon and Kyle had noticed that Tim was a doubter and complainer. He was hardly ever pleased about anything, and he questioned everything a person said.

"How in the world can you tell anything is missing, when you have so much food and are preparing meals three times a day?" Milk complained.

Dillon and Kyle spoke up as well: "It wasn't us. We know the rules and haven't touched a thing."

Then all eyes went to Ralph. He liked to eat and was a little on the husky side. He would have made a good bully, but he was too nice for that. In fact, he had a sense of humor, although you didn't dare pick on him. "Well, don't look at me!" he said. "I didn't take any food."

Another boy on board was Bobby. He was a nice boy, but he was very gullible. The crew found they could get him to believe

just about anything, so they liked to play practical jokes on him. "I wouldn't think of stealing food," he said. "I've always been taught that it is wrong to steal."

"Well, someone is taking food, and I have ways of finding out who it is," Cookie warned.

Days went by, and the food kept disappearing from the galley pantry. Cookie tried to catch the thief several times but couldn't figure out how someone was taking the food without being noticed. He even locked the galley door at night, only to find food still missing.

Dillon and Kyle were talking to Cookie about it one afternoon. "Cookie, we don't know who's taking the snacks, but I think we have a way to catch him red-handed," Dillon said confidently.

"Really? How's that?"

"We don't know who it is, do we?" Kyle asked.

"Of course not."

"And we don't know when or how he is sneaking into the galley, right?" Dillon added.

"Right. I don't know that either," said

Cookie. "If I knew that, I'd have caught him by now. Get to the point. I've got lunch to prepare."

"What is it the thief takes more than anything else?" asked Kyle.

"Well, he likes the cookies, but the potato chips seem to be his favorite."

"Can we borrow a bag of chips?" asked Dillon.

"Sure."

"And we need one other special item," coaxed Kyle.

"What's that?"

"Come closer, and we'll tell you."

Cookie and the boys formed a huddle as Dillon and Kyle whispered their plan quietly. Keeping a close lookout for spies, they unveiled their little surprise.

"Boys, I'm proud of you. That is the best plan I think I've ever heard. We'll do it tonight."

Cookie, Dillon and Kyle set up the trap that afternoon. Everything was locked up as usual. And they gave no appearance of what they were doing, nor did they tell anyone else of their masterful plan.

Well, kids, I'll finish this story right after the Bible lesson and tell you how they caught the "potato chip bandit," if you listen closely.

Boys and girls, ever since the beginning of creation, men and women have been trying to hide their sins. Adam and Eve were the very first when they tried to hide from the presence of God. Then Cain tried to hide his sin by pretending he didn't know about it. A man by the name of Achan hid his sin in the sand under his tent. No matter how it is done, trying to hide sin is pointless, because God can see beyond the hiding place.

In our story, the potato chip bandit was stealing from the galley pantry. He failed to realize that he was the one being robbed. "How is that?" you ask.

First, stealing robs you of righteousness. "Righteousness" means doing right. In Exodus 20:15, the Bible says, "Thou shalt not steal." Stealing is a sin. We all have the opportunity to live a righteous life or an unrighteous one. When we steal, we sin against others as well as God.

God hates it when we are dishonest. Proverbs 11:1 says, "A false balance is abomination to the LORD: but a just weight is his delight." In Bible times, when a person sold some corn to someone else, he would weigh it with a scale. A dishonest merchant would use "false" weights and cheat the customer—in other words, he was stealing from them. God says that is an "abomination," something He hates.

Second, stealing robs you of giving. In Ephesians 4:28 the Bible tells us, "Let him that stole steal no more: but rather let him labour, working with his hands the thing which is good, that he may have to give to him that needeth."

God wants us to work honestly for our wages. Why? That we may give to others. We are not to be takers but givers. Jesus said that it is better to give than to receive. Giving is an attribute of God, and it is the way to be happy.

Third, stealing robs God of glory. The word "glory" means a good reputation. First Peter 4:15 states, "But let none of you suffer as a murderer, **or as a thief,** or as an evildoer, or as a busybody in other men's matters."

Our lifestyle can say either good or bad things about God. People judge our God by the way we live. When we steal, we lose our testimony to the unsaved. If we are dishonest in other things, who is going to believe us when we share the gospel story? A poor testimony tells others that our faith is not worth having.

So it is important to be honest. You see, when you steal, you take more than money or things.

✮✮✮

The day declined into sunset, and sunset, to bedtime. Dillon and Kyle went to bed as usual, but when it appeared the other boys were asleep, they sneaked out of the sleeping berth and made their way to the deck above and over toward the galley. Outside the galley several lifeboats were mounted and covered with a tarp. Carefully, they climbed inside a lifeboat with Cookie and quietly waited. They peeked out from underneath the tarp toward the galley, trying to remain undetected.

An hour went by, and no one even came near the galley door. "I don't think this is going to work," whispered Cookie.

"Maybe you're right. Even so, it might take all night waiting like this," said Dillon.

Kyle added, "We'll wait another—"

Before he could get the words out, they heard their homemade alarm—a snap and a loud scream! Then there was some stumbling around, with pots, pans and tin cans clanging inside the galley.

The three detectives ran to the galley and threw open the door. Cookie flipped on the light switch in order to see who the potato chip bandit was. By then several members of the evening watch had arrived to see what the commotion was all about.

"What's going on in here?" they demanded.

When they looked inside, they found the

culprit tangled in pots, pans and tin cans, which were tied together with string. "It bit me! It bit me!" he screamed in horror.

Soon the whole crew had gathered at the door and were laughing their heads off at the funny sight. There was Milk in the tangled string, and on the tips of three fingers, a mouse-trap. The little surprise had done its work.

"So you're the one who's been stealing the food," Cookie confirmed aloud. They also could see how he got inside the galley. A secret panel connected the galley to the

bathroom. Milk had discovered it one day and told no one about it. The panel slid to the side, which allowed him to sneak inside the galley, take his stolen treasure and leave without being noticed.

"That's not fair! That's not fair!" he cried. Now that he realized he was caught, he was desperate to put the blame on someone else.

"What's not fair is that you were stealing our food," replied Cookie.

"I wasn't stealing it," he argued. "I was only borrowing it. I was going to replace it."

"Well, since you were borrowing it and since you were going to replace it," Cookie went on, "I'll let you pay for it by working extra hours in the galley."

"That's not fair!"

"And since you like potatoes so much, you can peel them for the next two weeks."

So each day for the next two weeks, when Milk was not on a watch, he entered the galley and peeled potatoes while Cookie prepared the meal.

Chapter 4
Anchors Aweigh

"Ding-ding, ding-ding, ding-ding," rang out the ship's bell.

"How many bells was that?" Kyle's eyes were only half-opened.

Six bells sounded out into the sleeping quarters, waking up the crew. It meant it was seven o'clock in the morning and time to get out of the sack, dress and go to breakfast before the day of training began.

"Don't tell me it's time to get up already," moaned Dillon, as he struggled to open his eyes.

"Yes, it is!" shouted Mr. Riggs. "Now get

out of your sacks and get dressed! We've got something important to tell you topside right after breakfast."

It was unusual for Mr. Riggs to come into the crew quarters at all, let alone in such a temper.

"Really, Mr. Riggs? What is it?" questioned Kyle.

"You'll find out soon enough," Mr. Riggs growled. "Now get on with you, or I'll feed the whole lot of you to the barnacles!"

"Aye, aye, Sir," the crew replied diligently.

Soon the entire crew had dressed and was sitting at the breakfast table with Cookie.

"Hey, Cookie, what's up?" asked Ralph.

"I don't know. It could be just about anything from scrubbing the decks for the captain's inspection to setting sail."

The recruits soon found that the captain's inspection was no fun at all. It required every square inch of the ship to be spotless. He would check every nook and cranny—even places only the spiders and mice knew existed.

"I hope we don't have to spend another day mopping and dusting," grumbled Milk. "I'm starting to think we're being trained to be maids instead of sailors."

Everyone chuckled except Bobby. He was from the country, a little naïve and gullible when it came to practical jokes. "Do you really think so?" he asked with concern.

"That isn't what I heard," answered Charles. "I heard that we're gonna be tested on sailing today."

"Really?" Bobby looked around anxiously at the other boys.

"Yeah, and if we fail, we will be made to walk the plank, blindfolded."

"Really?" Bobby said again, gulping.

"Yup, right into the water, clothes and all."

By now everyone knew Charles was pulling Bobby's leg.

"I heard from the sailors that when a boot failed the test last year, they tied him to the top mast for two days without food or water," added Ralph.

"Yeah, and the sea gulls began to eat him before they could take him down," said Kyle. "Now his ghost roams the ship in the middle of the night, reciting the ship's manual. In fact, I think I saw him making his way to your bunk last night, Bobby."

"Stop! You guys are scaring me."

With that, they began to laugh. "They're just kidding, Bobby," assured Cookie. "It's probably nothing at all. Now you fellas eat your breakfast and get ready for the captain. And be sure to look sharp!"

Eight bells sounded. The officer of the deck, sounding out the boatswain's whistle, called the crew amidships to stand at attention.

"OU-EE-AH," blew the call.

Each man stood in his place as Captain Blair made his way to the crew. Once again the boatswain's whistle was sounded, alerting the crew that the captain was getting ready to address them.

Each man stood at attention. Mr. Riggs eyed the formation to be sure they were at proper attention and dressed appropriately.

"Good morning, men," spoke the captain. "I'm pleased to announce that each of our new boots are progressing nicely. Thanks to Mr. Riggs and Mr. Jars, the training is ahead of schedule. That means that at nine hundred hours we are going to take a short trip out of the harbor to see how each one handles the ship while under sail. We will anchor a short way out into the bay and evaluate your progress."

The new recruits did all they could to keep from shouting for joy! They realized the day had finally arrived when they would actually sail.

"All of you know your duties and assignments. It is important that the boots as well as the sailors attend to their posts with diligence. I'm counting on the sailors to keep an eye out for the recruits, seeing that it is their first time out. I know I can count on them. Boots, I'm counting on you to pay attention, follow orders immediately and do as you've been taught."

Captain Blair looked over to Mr. Riggs and gave the command, "Prepare the crew for setting sail, Mr. Riggs."

"Aye, aye, Sir. Prepare the crew for setting sail," he repeated.

The captain then walked slowly to the poop deck as Mr. Riggs dismissed the crew and gave them orders to be ready to set sail at the strike of two bells.

"All right!" Kyle exclaimed excitedly. "This is going to be fantastic!"

"I know," Dillon replied, as they hurriedly walked to their quarters to change into working uniforms. The entire crew was talking enthusiastically as they anticipated their first trip out while under sail.

"Ding-ding," sounded the brass bell.

The crew was already waiting for their orders. The captain stood atop the poop deck, looking toward the bow of the ship. "Heave up the anchor, Mr. Riggs, and get under way at once," he commanded.

With each order, Mr. Riggs would respond with an "aye, aye, Sir" and then would repeat the command to the crew. The crew would then repeat the order if they were to carry out the task.

"Man the capstan," called Mr. Riggs.

"Man the capstan, Sir!" called out those who were to haul up the anchor.

Six of the crew members were to stand around a hub with six bars projecting from it, much like an old wagon wheel with spokes coming out of it. As they pushed against the bars and began walking forward in circles, the cable of the anchor began to wrap around the hub.

Soon the music of the pawls could be heard, "clank, clank, clank," as the cable made its way into the ship, pulling the anchor out of the mud and freeing it from its hold.

"Heave away, my Johnnies!" cried out Mr. Riggs.

Mr. Jars put his hands to his mouth and trumpeted up to the captain, "Anchor's aweigh, Sir!" That meant the anchor was free from its hold on the harbor bottom but not yet all the way up into the ship.

"Very well, Sir!" answered Captain Blair. "Send a couple of men aloft to loose the course and topsails, and heave up your anchor."

"Aye, aye, Sir!" answered Mr. Riggs, and in

the same breath ordered, "Heave up the capstan!"

The crew answered this with, "Heave away the capstan, Sir!"

"Send a couple of men aloft, Mr. Jars," Mr. Riggs called out to the second mate.

"Aye, aye, Sir!" answered Mr. Jars. "Jump aloft, you sailors, and take the gaskets off the sails."

"Aye, aye, Sir!" they answered, and two men for each mast scrambled up the rigging like monkeys.

"One of you go aft and take the wheel!" he continued.

"Take the wheel, Sir!" answered another.

Soon the pilot called to the captain, "Give her the jibs, Sir!" That meant that the ship was ready to sail and that the jib sails could be dropped from the yardarms, allowing the wind to push the ship forward.

"Set the jibs, Mr. Riggs!" the captain commanded.

"Set the jibs, Sir!" he at once replied. "Jib halyards, a couple of you! Up with the flying jib and jib topsail, also!"

This was Dillon and Kyle's job, so they replied, "Set the jibs, Sir!"

The boys began to heave, or pull, on the lines which pulled the jib sails into the breeze. As the sails were being let out, they cracked and flapped in the wind.

Dillon and Kyle were full of pride as they performed their tasks. Gradually, the ship began to plow through the water as other sails were let out into the wind. The boys looked over to the starboard and noticed that a crowd of people had formed on shore and were observing the ship being put under sail.

"Man, is this ever exciting!" exclaimed Dillon, a big grin on his face.

"I'll say!" replied Kyle. "I could never have imagined how exciting this would be."

Orders continued to be given, the crew obeyed the commands, and soon the ship was pulling out from the harbor and into the bay under full sail. It was the most beautiful sight and experience the boys had ever witnessed. Straight ahead the clear sky and bright sun beckoned, as if to say, "Follow me."

This reminds me of Proverbs 4:18:

"The path of the just is as the shining light, that shineth more and more unto the perfect day."

This means those who trust in God are on a path to greater things. The sailing adventure was just beginning, and the boys had great anticipation for greater things. The "shining light" this verse speaks about is the truth of God's Word. The way our path gets brighter is by putting the Bible into practice.

We must do more than just get saved. We must be a follower of Jesus and His Word. As Dillon and Kyle got on board the *SkipJack* and learned how to sail her, we must learn the ways of God.

Let me give you some ways in which we can begin a path of greater things in the Christian life.

First, we must get disciplined in the

Christian life. Paul stressed this in I Corinthians 9:24–27:

"Know ye not that they which run in a race run all, but one receiveth the prize? So run, that ye may obtain.

"And every man that striveth for the mastery is temperate in all things. Now they do it to obtain a corruptible crown; but we an incorruptible.

"I therefore so run, not as uncertainly; so fight I, not as one that beateth the air:

"But I keep under my body, and bring it into subjection: lest that by any means, when I have preached to others, I myself should be a castaway."

Discipline is the process of orderly, controlled conduct in order to mold, correct and perfect one's character. Character determines one's outcome in life. If you have positive character traits, you can aspire to great things in society, life and God's work. God determines what will help us become disciplined, just as the captain of the *SkipJack* determined what would make good sailors. Jesus is our Captain, and the

Bible is our manual of discipline.

Second, we must get educated about Jesus Christ. The boys found that the more they learned about the ship, the better they could function in its operation. The apostle Paul told Timothy:

"Continue thou in the things which thou hast learned and hast been assured of, knowing of whom thou hast learned them;

"And that from a child thou hast known the holy scriptures, which are able to make thee wise unto salvation through faith which is in Christ Jesus."—II Timothy 3:14,15.

Paul understood the importance of living according to the Scriptures, allowing God's truth to guide us to a brighter future.

Third, we must get skilled in living for God. Notice the promise of a good path when we apply the biblical principles found in Proverbs 2:1-9:

"My son, if thou wilt receive my words, and hide my commandments with thee;

"So that thou incline thine ear unto wisdom, and apply thine heart to understanding;

"Yea, if thou criest after knowledge, and liftest up thy voice for understanding;

"If thou seekest her as silver, and searchest for her as for hid treasures;

"Then shalt thou understand the fear of the LORD, and find the knowledge of God.

"For the LORD giveth wisdom: out of his mouth cometh knowledge and understanding.

"He layeth up sound wisdom for the righteous: he is a buckler to them that walk uprightly.

"He keepeth the paths of judgment, and preserveth the way of his saints.

"Then shalt thou understand righteousness, and judgment, and equity; yea, every good path."

Being skilled in the Christian life requires that we learn it and practice it. The more we live out the principles of God, the better we will get at living for God. It is not always fun and exciting to practice; it takes discipline and character to become a good sailor for Jesus. Will you strive to become that type of Christian?

"Take her to starboard and into the bay,

Mr. Norman," shouted the captain to the navigator.

"Aye, aye, Sir!" he responded. "Take her to starboard."

"To starboard, Sir," repeated the helmsman.

The ship began to turn to the right and into the bay's center. She sailed gently through the water, passing by smaller boats of all kinds. There were motorboats, yachts and sailboats scattered through the bluish-green waters. The *SkipJack* was the queen

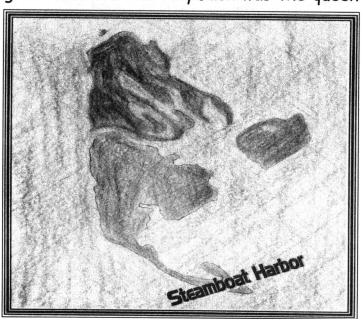

Steamboat Harbor

of the waterway as every person eyed her.

She moved south through the Chesapeake Bay for nine hours, until they neared the headwaters of Virginia, and then anchored near a little island called Tangier.

"Captain John Smith stopped here in 1608 to look for fresh water," Mr. Norman said to the boys as they sat at supper. "He traveled as far as Washington, D.C., in order to find more settlements."

"Wow! That's really neat," said Kyle.

"I also read that he was badly stung by a stingray and had to return to Jamestown to be treated," Mr. Norman continued.

"Mr. Norman, do you think we'll stay here long?" asked Bobby.

"The crew all performed very well, so I think once we pick up some fresh supplies in Tangier, we'll set sail in a couple of days."

Each recruit knew what that meant. The ship would take them into the Atlantic Ocean, into the deep waters. The harbor and bay waters were easy to navigate. The Atlantic would be another story.

Anchors Aweigh

After supper, the crew members were able to relax for the rest of the evening. The boys sat near the bow of the ship and watched as the sun began to set over the horizon.

"Do you think we're ready for the deep waters?" Kyle asked Dillon, who was basking in the warm breeze and the beautiful evening sights.

"I think we are, but I have my reservations as to whether or not we can do it. I guess we'll find out soon enough—soon enough indeed!"

Chapter 5
Operation Tangier

The next morning the members of the USS *SkipJack* were told they could go ashore Tangier Island for a little rest and relaxation. They could visit some of the stores and purchase anything they might need for the three-week journey ahead.

"What do you think we could do?" asked Dillon, adjusting his cap in the mirror.

"I want to purchase some candy and toothpaste," Kyle replied. "I'm not really sure what they have on the island. Maybe we can even find some information about Captain John Smith."

"Yeah, that would be sweet! I even heard

that the pirate Blackbeard hid some treasure around here somewhere."

"Really?" Kyle asked enthusiastically.

"That's right. If we have time, maybe we can look for it!"

The boys made their way to amidships in order to board the whaleboats that were in position to receive those crew members going ashore. Even Mr. Riggs and Mr. Jars were going along. They seemed to be in a good mood and excited for the brief break away from their duties on board ship.

When the boat was filled to capacity, Mr. Riggs commanded the pilot to "shove off."

"Aye, aye, Sir," replied the sailor. With that, he started the little motor attached to the stern, and soon the boat was puttering its way to shore.

"It sure is fine out today," Dillon commented. "I think we'll have a great time since the weather is so nice."

"I agree," replied Kyle. "I wonder if they have souvenirs and stuff that I can purchase for my family."

"I'm sure they do. That reminds me, I need to buy a disposable camera so I can take pictures of our trip ashore."

Dillon and Kyle's short trip to shore was filled with lots of chatter and laughter. Sea gulls skimming the waves and soaring overhead seemed to escort the crew to the docks, which were crowded with people and busy with excitement. While some came to view the sights, others were preparing for a day of fishing.

"Mr. Drake said we could do some fishing off the side of the *SkipJack* once we get out a ways into the Atlantic Ocean," said Kyle.

"Really?"

"That's right. He said we'd see all kinds of fish out in the deep waters. We can catch any type of fish we want."

"Wow! I hope I catch a whale or something," said Dillon.

Kyle nearly choked with laughter. "Why not try for something bigger, like a sea monster!"

"Well, I guess a whale is a little too much," Dillon grinned. "Maybe I'd better start out with a flounder."

"That sounds like a good idea."

The boat pulled up to the dock, and a sailor jumped onto the pier, tying off the boat to the cleats.

"Everybody out!" shouted Mr. Riggs. "Be sure to be back here at fourteen hundred hours. If you're not here, you'll have to swim back to the ship!"

"Let's go over to that blue-colored shop," Kyle suggested, pointing toward the street lined with stores.

"Sounds good to me," replied Dillon. "It

looks like a good place for souvenirs. It sure has a funny name though, doesn't it?"

"Yeah. Whoever thought of the name 'Captain Shell's Seaside Seclusional'?"

"I don't know. They must have been born with tongue-twisting tonsils to tickle trout toward Tuesday," said Dillon with a grin.

They both laughed at that little tongue twister.

When the boys entered the store, a jingling of bells sounded, letting the employees know that someone had entered. Dillon and Kyle looked around and noticed aisles of shelves loaded with all kinds of things: fishing gear, snacks, boat supplies and, of course, lots of souvenirs. There was even a little soda fountain and food counter where you could sit down to eat sandwiches or drink a soda.

"Hey, check this out!" said Dillon. "It's a brass-plated fish finder for only a dollar."

"Let me see," said Kyle, as he turned around to check it out. "Real funny! That's nothing more than a pack of fishing hooks!"

Dillon just laughed.

"Quit fooling around! We've got to get serious if we're going to find everything we need before the day is out," coaxed Kyle, even though he did think it was pretty funny.

As they were busy looking through all the things, they heard a familiar voice—or at least somewhat familiar.

"We zullen elkaar by de vergader plaats ontmoeten. Als we bij Razor Pass zijn kunnen we ons plan uitvoeren."

"Wow! Who is that talking funny?" asked Kyle. "It sounds like Martian language."

The boys were able to peek through a crack in one of the shelves to see three men. The only thing the boys could see was the backs of the uniforms from their waist up to their necks. They were talking as though they were trying to keep a secret.

"Hey, two of those guys are wearing *SkipJack* uniforms," said Dillon. "I didn't know any of our guys spoke another language. I wonder what they are saying."

"Beats me," replied Kyle seriously. "The only thing I understood was Razor Pass and somebody's Aunt Moo who weighs a ton."

"Can you get a look at who it is?" asked Dillon.

"No, I can't. I can't see their heads, only their backs from the shoulders down. Let's go over and take a look."

The boys began to walk around the counter. As they were walking around the end of the aisle, a shelf came loose from its hold. "Look out!" yelled Kyle.

All the items came tumbling down in front of them. Before they knew it, the store

employees had rushed to the scene. One, about forty years old, appeared to be the store manager. "What are you doing over here?" he demanded.

"We're not doing anything, Sir," answered Dillon carefully. "We were just walking around the corner when the shelf came loose. We didn't touch a thing."

"So, you mean to tell me that stuff came down all by itself?"

"Yes, Sir. That's exactly what we're saying," added Kyle. "We didn't touch anything. We came around the corner, and then it all fell down—honest."

"Those shelves are locked in. There is no way one of them would have fallen without someone messing around with it. Now who did it?"

"I'm telling you, we didn't touch it. It fell just as we got to the end of the aisle," Dillon protested.

"Well, you need to be more careful, or just leave," said the manager disgustedly, not believing anything they said.

"Okay, we'll just leave and shop somewhere else. But we didn't do it," stated Dillon.

Soon the boys were out of the store. "I can't believe they didn't believe us," said Kyle.

"I know," added Dillon. "That's okay; we didn't want to buy any of their junk anyhow!"

"That's right. Captain Shell can keep his junk! Hey, we didn't get a chance to see who the crew members were in the store."

The boys walked over to the store's display window and peered inside.

"I don't see anyone in there now," Dillon said.

"Me neither. They must have left while the commotion was going on."

"Yeah, you're right. I did hear the bells on the door jingle when we were being accused. Well, we can find out later. Besides, it doesn't really matter. Let's go over to the other store across the street."

"Which one?" asked Kyle.

"How about the Blue Dolphin? The sign says, 'You'uns need it; We'uns got it. From blubber oil to crab sauce.'"

"With a sign like that, they've gotta have what we need! Let's go!" Kyle said. "The last one to the door is a rotten egg," he challenged, as he began to dart across the street.

The boys spent the rest of the day checking out the island, purchasing the supplies they needed and taking pictures. The day seemed to hurry by as they enjoyed the sights and sounds of Tangier Island. It wasn't long before they were back at the dock, waiting for the whaleboat to take them back to the ship. Others gathered until all were there.

"Hey, which of you guys speaks a foreign language?" asked Kyle.

Everyone just looked at them. "What are you talking about," asked Mr. Riggs.

"Dillon and I were in a store and heard some of our crew mates speaking in another language," Kyle answered. "It's no big deal; we were just wondering, that's all."

"Well, lots of guys do; now mind your own business," he growled.

"I wonder what his problem is," Dillon whispered to Kyle.

"I don't know. He must have had some thistle pudding at Captain Shell's."

"What are you whispering about?" Mr. Riggs questioned sharply, glaring at them.

"Oh, nothing, nothing at all, Sir," answered Kyle.

"Everyone in the boat, and be quick about it!" shouted Mr. Riggs.

As the boat began to motor away toward the USS *SkipJack*, the crew was strangely quiet. Perhaps they were afraid to say anything. Or perhaps they knew something that Dillon and Kyle didn't. As the boat made its way through the one-foot waves, the boys wondered why Mr. Riggs was so touchy.

☆☆☆

Well, boys and girls, I'll let you know what conclusion the boys came up with right after the Bible lesson. This reminds me of a passage of Scripture, II Timothy 1:12:

"For the which cause I also suffer these things: nevertheless I am not ashamed: for I know whom I have believed, and am persuaded that he is able to keep that which I

have committed unto him against that day."

Dillon and Kyle ran into several situations that were not planned. They found themselves being accused for something they didn't do. Their day began with good intentions but ended in turmoil.

Many times we will find ourselves faced with situations and problems that were not planned. Sometimes things happen that we wish would go away, but they are real and present. What should we do? Get upset and yell? Sit around and worry? Turn mean and yell at everyone? Of course we shouldn't.

I think the boys did the right thing, don't you? They committed the situation (turned it over) to God. I think you'll agree with me that there are some things we need to commit or turn over to God.

First, we should commit our souls to God. Our souls are eternal. We will either have eternal life with God or eternal Hell with Satan. You will live forever somewhere. When this body passes away, the eternal soul lives on. Paul said that he wasn't ashamed of Jesus, because He had committed his soul to Him for eternal life in Heaven.

Did you ever get an A on a test? When you are given a grade for your schoolwork, the teacher is committed to keep your grade secure. You don't worry about it; you don't have to do anything to keep it an A. Once it is recorded, it is permanent.

Once we trust Christ as our Saviour, it is up to Him to keep us. It can't be changed. It is permanent. Paul believed God would keep His promise about salvation.

Second, we should commit our ways unto God. What way is that? It is our future. Do you know that God has a great plan for your future? Jeremiah, chapter 29, tells us that plan is one of peace and happiness:

"For I know the thoughts that I think toward you, saith the LORD, thoughts of peace, and not of evil, to give you an expected end.

"Then shall ye call upon me, and ye shall go and pray unto me, and I will hearken unto you."—Vss. 11,12.

When Dillon and Kyle were in the store, the shelf fell. Everything was a mess. Sometimes life is like that. You get in trouble for something or do something that messes everything up, and then you can't change it.

God is saying that He doesn't see that as your permanent way of life. He wants "to give you an expected end." In other words, He wants to straighten up everything. Until that happens, trust Him. Call upon God and pray. Commit the mess to God and let Him work it out.

Why should you do that? Because He has "thoughts of peace, and not of evil" toward you. God's plan is not to make your life more miserable. He sincerely wants to help you. What He is asking you to do is commit it to Him, turn it over to Him.

That is the wonderful thing about God. He loves us even when we don't love ourselves. He cares for our future even when we think things are unfixable.

The next time you get in a jam, go to God in prayer. Talk to Him and then look for His direction.

"Do you know what, Dillon?"

"Yeah, I think I do. Are you thinking what I'm thinking?"

"I don't know. What are you thinking?" Kyle asked.

"I'm thinking something fishy is going on. I mean, it's a little odd that we heard some of our guys speaking another language and—"

"And then no one 'fessing up to it," interrupted Kyle.

"That's right. And then that shelf—"

"Falling down just as we were rounding the corner," interrupted Kyle again.

"Yeah. Then when we began to ask a few questions—"

"We get yelled at by Mr. Riggs," Kyle finished once more.

"Exactly!" Dillon agreed.

The boys looked at each other. "Do you think it means anything?" asked Kyle.

"I don't know, but I say, let's do a little investigating when we get back to the ship."

"That's a good idea. We'll just keep it to ourselves," said Kyle. "We can call it 'Operation Tangier.'"

"I like that—Operation Tangier. Who knows, maybe it's nothing," said Dillon guardedly, "but then on the other hand—"

Kyle couldn't help but cut in, "—maybe something rotten is going on!"

"Exactly!"

Chapter 6
Secrets of the Hold

The next day food and supplies arrived by boat to the USS *SkipJack*. The crew began to load the supplies in various parts of the ship.

"Hurry along there, boots!" commanded Mr. Riggs. "We want to set sail tomorrow."

"Mr. Riggs, what time do you think we'll get underway?" Dillon asked.

"Hopefully, right after breakfast. If we get everything loaded, stowed away and shipshape, we should have no problem. We need to get a good start tomorrow. We want to be sure to make it to Razor Pass by Thursday."

The boys looked at each other, stunned by what Mr. Riggs had just said.

"Did you say Razor Pass?" Dillon asked.

"Yeah, Razor Pass. What's wrong? You look like you just saw a green-tailed mermaid!"

"Oh, nothing, Mr. Riggs," replied Kyle, who quickly thought of an explanation to cover up their real thoughts. "I guess...well, I guess it sounds dangerous, that's all."

"It can be dangerous, but don't worry.

We've made it through the pass many times before without any problems. It's just important that everyone stay on his toes. Besides, it's several weeks away, and we still have time to learn those skills."

"That's good to know, Sir," said Dillon slowly.

Mr. Riggs turned away sharply toward another mate. "Hey there! Put that box in the forecastle storage," he said, as he walked away from the boys. Mr. Riggs spent most of the day giving orders as to where things went.

"Hey, Dillon and Kyle," called Mr. Riggs.

"Coming, Sir," they both shouted, as they ran to the side of Mr. Riggs.

"I want you boys to go to the hold of the ship and see if you can find a yellow storage box for me. It will have a sticker on its side that says '**HARDWARE**.'"

"Aye, aye, Sir," Dillon replied.

"What should we do with it when we find it?" asked Kyle.

"Take it to Mr. Royce, who will use what's

inside. Now off with you, because he needs it right away." Mr. Royce was the ship's carpenter who not only made new parts for the ship but also made repairs.

"Aye, aye, Sir," they replied. Then, with a turning on their heels, both headed off to get a flashlight, since it was dark in the hold. Next, they went to the ladder stairs leading into the bottom of the ship.

The *SkipJack* had several decks: the main deck, the second deck and the first deck. The main deck was on the very top of the ship, exposed to the elements. An enclosed partial deck at the rear of the ship was called the poop deck, a name which comes from a French word meaning "to come over the top of something." The elevated portion of the main deck at the bow, or front, of the ship is called the forecastle.

The second deck, located beneath the main deck, housed the galley and sleeping quarters for Cookie, the captain and officers of the *SkipJack*. It also housed a workshop for the ship's carpenter and storage for the ship's rigging.

The first deck was converted into the sleeping quarters for the crew and housed the bathrooms and showers.

The hold of a ship was at one time used by the ancient tall ships to store their cargo. They would transport cargo from port to port, much like tractor-trailer trucks do today. Since the *SkipJack* was no longer used for that purpose, the hold was used to keep the many supplies needed for her trips.

"Man, is this place spooky, or what?" said Dillon, looking cautiously around for anything suspicious.

"You're right," affirmed Kyle. "I don't like the idea of stepping on a big rat, or a foot-long cockroach either."

"I don't know how we'll find anything with all these supplies down here," added Dillon.

"Hey, quiet!" whispered Kyle. "I think someone is down here."

"Yeah, so what?" Dillon quipped unconcernedly. Then he lifted his arms and began to imitate a ghost, saying in a spooky voice, "Unless you think it's a ghost. O-o-o-o-o-o-h-h-h-h," he concluded with a big laugh.

"No, I don't," Kyle whispered. "But maybe we can get them to think *we* are," he continued with a grin.

"That would be funny," Dillon snickered. "Let's try it."

They hunched down and began to sneak over toward the bow of the ship in the direction of the voices. "I think they're just on the other side of these boxes," Kyle said quietly. "On the count of three, we'll jump out and yell."

Before Kyle began counting, the voices became clearer. Both boys froze and listened intently from behind the main mast that was resting on top of the keel beam. "I think it's that foreign language again," whispered Kyle.

"Can you hear what they're saying?" asked Dillon quietly.

"We **moeten** very careful be, **dat** we put **dit plan** together properly. Each of us has to do our **taak** just right, or we'll **noit** pull this off," one voice said.

"**Ja,** we want her not sink, **all-lain-maar** cripple her," said another man.

"**Ja, dat's** right," said a third. "We'll **zien** the boss at Razor Pass and get more of the **day teye uhs.**"

The boys looked at each other, wide-eyed as they realized they had stumbled upon something big.

"We need to get a look at who these guys are," Dillon said softly. "Let's head back to the stern and get out of here. We can watch who comes up from the second deck."

The two began to move toward the stern of the ship, carefully walking around the boxes and supplies. As they got near the stairway leading to the first deck, Dillon

tripped over one of the hull joists and fell into a crate of pump parts. The crate broke open, scattering nuts, bolts and parts in every direction. It made quite a racket, and Dillon let out a big, "Ouch!"

"Hey, who's **dat!**" shouted one of the men.

"Let's get out of here!" commanded Kyle. And with that, they stumbled up the ladder as fast as they could. They could hear the men climbing over boxes and tripping along the way as they chased after the boys.

"Let's get them!" one shouted.

"**Ja!** Don't let them get away!" shouted another.

Dillon and Kyle made their way to the crew bathrooms and hid out in one of the stalls.

They heard one of the men outside the bathroom say, "Let's spread out and see if we can tell who it was." Then they heard footsteps going off in different directions and out of earshot.

"Something isn't right about all of this," huffed Kyle.

"You're telling me! Something is definitely

up. I think we stumbled upon a theft ring or something."

"It sounds like they want to sabotage the *SkipJack* for some reason," said Kyle. "But why would they want to do that?"

"Maybe they're pirates and plan to over-throw the ship near this place called Razor Pass," suggested Dillon.

"Operation Tangier is now officially under way," announced Kyle.

"Maybe we should tell Captain Blair," proposed Dillon.

"I think he would just laugh at us because we don't have any proof. No, we'd better wait until we get more evidence and at least find out what they're up to."

The boys waited about twenty minutes for the search to die down and made their way down into the hold once again to retrieve the yellow box they were ordered to find. Then they took it to Mr. Royce, who was a little perturbed about getting the box so late. But soon all was smoothed over, and the *SkipJack* was prepared to get under way the next morning.

The boys went to bed that night anticipating their trip into the Atlantic and wondering what this Razor Pass thing was all about.

Dillon and Kyle's experience reminds me of a man who fell asleep in a ship's hold. His name was Jonah, an Old Testament prophet who had a job to do for the Lord but who decided to disobey. He bought a ticket to sail on a ship going in the opposite direction from where God had told him to go.

What is odd about Jonah's story is that while he was sleeping in the hold of the ship, a storm was brewing above. The Bible tells us that God sent the storm because of Jonah's disobedience.

The frightened sailors believed that someone on board was responsible for the storm. They soon found it was Jonah's fault. The sailors questioned him about why God would do this. When Jonah told them he was running from God, they asked another question. It was simple and direct: "Why hast thou done this?" (Jonah 1:10). In other words, "Jonah, what made you think you could run from God and get away with it?"

That is a good question, isn't it? Why is it that we turn from God and attempt to go our own way? What makes us think we can run from God and live without Him? The reason is found in Jonah 2:8: "They that observe lying vanities forsake their own mercy."

The word "observe" means to spend time thinking about a lie. Jonah's problem was that he was lying to himself. He convinced himself what he was doing was right. He talked himself into believing there would be no harm done if he disobeyed. He made excuses why he should run from God. In fact, he did such a good job of it that he was able to sleep quite soundly in the hold of the ship in spite of the dangerous storm raging outside.

The phrase "lying vanities" has the idea of believing something that is not true. Not only is it not true, it is harmful. Just as the Easter bunny is a complete fabrication, so was Jonah's belief that he could run from God.

A lying vanity is a lie that hurts you. We must remember that sin is not only a disappointment to God but harmful to us.

The Devil is a master of lying and deceiving. In fact, Jesus called him "a liar" and "the father" of lies in John 8:44. Believe nothing the Devil tells you.

Not only that, but we can lie to ourselves. Proverbs 14:12 reads, "There is a way which seemeth right unto a man, but the end thereof are the ways of death."

The Bible plainly tells us we must be careful that what we tell ourselves is biblical.

What we learn from Jonah is, don't listen to lies. Don't try to make your sin sound like a good thing. We also learn that when we do make a big mistake like this, we need to pray for God's forgiveness. Then we need to keep our vow, or promise, to the Lord.

★★★

The ship got under way early the next morning, with every man at his post. The captain gave the order, "Heave up the anchor, Mr. Riggs."

"Aye, aye, Sir, heave up the anchor!" repeated Mr. Riggs.

"Set sail for Razor Pass."

"Set sail for Razor Pass, Sir," he repeated before giving the command to the crew.

It would take most of the day to get out of the Chesapeake Bay. By the next morning they would be traveling northward along the coast of Virginia and then along the coast of Maryland, Delaware, New Jersey and, finally, New York.

The boys were comfortable doing their jobs. They had dreamed of this day for a long time.

But what about the secrets they overheard in the hold of the ship? What would happen once they reached Razor Pass if they even got there? Would they find adventure or pirates?

Chapter 7
Navigation Nightmare

The USS *SkipJack* was sailing through the waters along the coastline of Delaware, and the new boots were putting their skills into action with precision. Dillon and Kyle were especially proud and were enjoying all the new sounds and smells of sailing on the ocean.

The boys were pulling on a halyard when they heard a familiar voice shouting to them: "Dillon! Kyle!"

"Yes, Captain Blair?" responded Kyle.

"Tie up the line on the pin and come here. I have something to tell you."

"Aye, aye, Sir!" they answered without hesitation and immediately went into action to secure the sail. Captain Blair was patiently waiting and observing how they tied off the line. It was important that each sailor learn the correct knots to secure the sails so they would not slip. He seemed pleased as Dillon wrapped the line on the belaying pin.

"You two will have a very special duty today."

"What's that, Captain?" quizzed Dillon anxiously.

"You will be going to the navigation room with Mr. Norman to learn how he navigates the ship."

A big grin spread across his face as Kyle exclaimed, "Fantastic!"

"Awesome!" Dillon asserted.

Captain Blair smiled as well, for he could remember the first time he had the opportunity to learn navigation aboard a tall ship. It was just as exciting today as it was then; he could relate to the excited boys.

"You had better get up there right away. He's waiting for you."

"Aye, aye, Captain," they answered in unison.

Turning on their heels, they scurried toward the wheelhouse. The only ones allowed in the wheelhouse were the officers and, of course, those learning navigation. It was off-limits to the crew, and you could go inside only if you were given special permission to do so.

"Reporting as ordered, Sir," Dillon said, as the two stood at attention.

"At ease, boys," Mr. Norman said kindly.

"While you are on duty in the wheelhouse, you will not need to be at attention or salute. We would not accomplish much if we were required to do that."

"Aye, aye, Sir," Kyle replied respectfully. "What should we do?"

"Come over here to the map table and take a look," Mr. Norman said, pointing to a large map that covered the tabletop.

On the map, they could see the coastline and the spot marking their location and course. Mr. Norman spent an hour explaining to the two boys how to plot courses, estimate travel times, find the depth of the waters and watch for dangers in the deep.

"If you'll notice on the map, there are lighthouses marked by these little dots. Each lighthouse has different blinking light patterns, which tell us exactly which light-house it is. That way, if it is dark outside, you can identify it by the way it blinks."

Mr. Norman told them about the differ-ent buoys in the water channels. There were red ones and green ones. If you were returning to land, the red ones would be on the starboard, or right, side. The green ones would be on the port, or left, side of the ship.

"How do you remember all of that stuff, Mr. Norman?" asked Kyle.

"It's quite simple. Just remember this simple saying: 'Red right returning.' In other words, keep the red to your right when you are returning from the sea."

"Oh, I get it!" said Dillon. "That really makes it simple."

"It sure does. If fact, when we come to Razor Pass next week, we'll have to keep that in mind, or we could be in danger."

Just the mention of Razor Pass sent chills down the boys' backs. They looked at each other and realized they had a great opportunity to bring up the subject. Kyle gave Dillon an elbow in the side in order to prod him into asking some questions.

"Ouch!" he mumbled, as the elbow went into his rib cage."

"What did you say, Dillon?" asked Mr. Norman.

"Oh, nothing, Sir. I mean...well...er...ah," he stammered.

"What is it?" Mr. Norman asked again.

"What he wants to know is, what exactly is this Razor Pass place you are talking about?" Kyle boldly asked. "We keep hearing about it but don't know much about it, except that it is a little dangerous to navigate."

"Yes, it is dangerous, but not to worry. We've done it many times. As long as each one stays alert and performs his duties, we'll have nothing to worry about."

"I've heard that before, but are there any foreigners?" Dillon asked cautiously, looking around the wheelhouse to make sure no one was listening.

"What do you mean, foreigners?" asked Mr. Norman.

"Well, I mean men from other countries outside the United States."

"No, not exactly. It is a part of New York State. But it's funny you should ask, because there will be a ship race near there. In fact, we're going to sail in the race along with several other countries."

The boys were stunned and fell silent as they looked at each other.

Mr. Norman, not noticing, pointed to a spot on the map and said, "Look here. Razor Pass is right here, and the race will take place a little bit north of there," he said, moving his finger to that location. "The winners will take home a trophy and fifty thousand dollars. They also get bragging rights and endorsements from businesses wanting to associate themselves with the winning ship. That can add up to millions of dollars."

"Fifty thousand dollars!" Kyle said loudly in astonishment. "I don't think I ever saw that much money before."

"It is a lot of money," Mr. Norman went on. "In fact, one time my grandfather—"

Dillon cut him off. "Other countries, you say," so as to coax more information from him and not lose their focus.

"That's right. There are ships from France, Australia, England, Spain and Holland. It's quite a sight to see all the beautiful ships at full sail, their flags waving in the wind."

"Wow, that does sound great!" exclaimed Kyle.

"And then we get to meet the sailors from around the world. Of course, it's hard to understand them, seeing they speak foreign languages."

Dillon realized this was another good opportunity to do some investigative questioning. "Mr. Norman, we heard some men on board our ship who were speaking another language. But we couldn't figure out what language it was."

"What did they say?" he asked.

Dillon replied, "I'm not sure, but the words sounded like, 'muton,' and 'noit.'"

"Yes, Sir, and then there was a 'Ja' and a 'dit plan,'" added Kyle.

"That sounds like Dutch," Mr. Norman went on. "We have several Dutch crew members on board."

"Really?" responded Dillon.

"Yes. In fact, we are fortunate to have them, because they are very good sailors. Some of the best, I might add. Their families have been sailors for hundreds of years. I think they have salt water in their veins."

With that, Mr. Norman continued his teaching about navigation and then eventually explained how the steering wheel worked. He must have taught them everything there was to know. He promised them both the opportunity to steer the ship right after lunch.

Trip of a Lifetime

Today ships of all sizes must learn how to navigate through the waters as well. Things have not really changed much over the past hundred years. There are still lighthouses, buoys, channel markers and rules to follow in order to avoid collision with other ships and water hazards. If a boat doesn't follow the red and green buoys placed in the water, it is in danger of getting stuck in shallow water. If a ship ignores the lighthouses, it is in danger of running aground and wrecking. If a captain ignores the rules of the waterways, he is in danger of hitting other ships or causing damage to shore properties.

Likewise, God has given us aids to navigating through life. Life has many dangers—dangers which can be avoided by following the rules of life.

Dillon and Kyle were excited to learn the navigation rules, for it gave them greater opportunities in sailing. The Bible gives us some important advice about being guided through the channels and oceans of life. Aids to navigation given to us by God will benefit us greatly. If we learn the rules of wisdom, we too can have freedom to do more things and enjoy life to its fullest. Hebrews 12:1

and 2 give us some good advice in this area:

"Wherefore seeing we also are compassed about with so great a cloud of witnesses, let us lay aside every weight, and the sin which doth so easily beset us, and let us run with patience the race that is set before us,

"Looking unto Jesus the author and finisher of our faith; who for the joy that was set before him endured the cross, despising the shame, and is set down at the right hand of the throne of God."

One thing found in waterways are markers, signs placed along channels and waterways to guide the way to a water source. Markers are numbered. The smaller the number, the closer you are to a port. The larger the number, the farther you are from a port.

Likewise, God has placed markers for us in this world. There are the markers of God's Word. Think of Bible verses as little markers. These guide us in several ways.

First, they guide us to Christ. Jesus said, "These are written, that ye might believe that Jesus is the Christ, the Son of God; and that believing ye might have life through his name" (John 20:31). God's Word will point us to Jesus. How could a person ever find God unless He showed them the way? Fortunately, God revealed the way of eternal life. If we follow His markers, they will lead us to Heaven.

Second, the markers reveal the danger of Satan. Like shallow waters and hidden rocks that can sink a ship, the Bible warns of dangers the Devil puts in our path. We are warned that we are to "put on the whole armour of God, that ye may be able to stand against the wiles of the devil" (Ephesians 6:11).

In I Peter 5:8 the Devil is compared to a lion waiting to devour us. He is at work trying to destroy our walk with God. The Bible shows us where he is hiding and how to be safe.

Lighthouses are another type of marker along the waterways. These tall towers rise high above the water and have a bright light at the top which can be seen for many miles. This gives the sailing ships a clear warning in the darkness from great distances.

Does God have lighthouses in the Bible? I can think of a very big one, described in John 3:14,15:

"As Moses lifted up the serpent in the wilderness, even so must the Son of man be lifted up:

"That whosoever believeth in him should not perish, but have eternal life."

Calvary's cross, with Jesus hanging between Heaven and earth, is like a lighthouse beaming out the message of salvation. The Bible tells us that we are in the darkness of sin. The only way to be saved from the rocks of sin is to trust Jesus as our Saviour. His death on the cross is like a lighthouse trying to get our attention. It points the way to Jesus, the true Saviour.

The lighthouse of Calvary says that if we don't heed the light of Jesus as our only way to Heaven, then we will wreck on the rocks of sin. The lighthouse doesn't point to any other way to salvation and safety, only Jesus.

The lighthouse did not go out when Jesus died on the cross; it only shone brighter, for Jesus rose from the dead three days later! It shines out the message, "Trust Jesus today!"

Another type of aid to navigation is a

buoy. Buoys are floating markers that are placed in the water and anchored to stay in that location. The ones who place the bouys have been that way before, so we can be sure that they marked a way of safe passage. Buoys are like white lines on a highway. They point a sailor in the right direction so he can stay on course. The surface of the ocean all looks pretty much the same, whether in the daytime or at night. The buoys are like arrows that direct the ships on the right course.

Does the Bible have buoys? Yes. They are called witnesses. Hebrews 12:1 says, "Wherefore seeing we also are compassed about with so great a cloud of witnesses..."

Pastors, teachers and parents who have already been where you are going are pointing you in the right direction, directing you around the dangers of life and showing you the safest way to travel. They are experienced in the pathways of life.

Let me urge you to put your faith in God's navigational aids and keep your eyes on Jesus and those "witnesses" who have gone before you.

✯✯✯

"Great!" Kyle blurted in delight. "My favorite lunch—dead dog stew!" This was another of Cookie's creations. He took the leftovers of the past week and mixed them together in a stew that actually tasted good. The only things that looked familiar were the big chunks of beef mixed with freshly caught and peeled shrimp. Beef gravy and rice completed the mixture.

"The waves are a little rough today, aren't they, Mr. Norman?" Dillon asked, digging his spoon into the stew.

"Yes, but not as bad as it can be. Sometimes the waves are four to five feet, and it gets a little wet on the main deck," he said with a chuckle.

"It looks like everyone is as hungry as we are," Kyle said, looking around the galley. "Hey, Cookie, what do you have for dessert?"

"Purple squid pie," he answered with a fiendish grin. "What you don't eat this afternoon, I'll use as bait to catch tonight's supper."

Although the names he gave to his dishes sounded quite awful, the recruits realized that it was all in jest. His cooking was almost as good as that of their mothers.

"Hey, boys," Mr. Norman called to Dillon and Kyle, "you were asking about those Dutch sailors this morning. Well, there they are, sitting at the far table on the right," pointing in their direction.

The boys looked where Mr. Norman was pointing and noticed six men sitting at the dinner table. None looked familiar, and the boys couldn't hear them talking very well. The Dutch sailors focused on eating and kept quiet. They certainly were not the

friendliest looking bunch of sailors.

It was then that Mr. Norman did something that scared the boys half to death. He called out loudly to the sailors, "Hey, Aifke, Fritz!"

The two responded with, "Ja, Mr. Norman?" The others also looked up and listened to what Mr. Norman was about to say.

"Dillon and Kyle here want to hear you speak some Dutch. They have an interest in Dutch sailors," he said with a grin. Unknowingly, Mr. Norman had just made the boys' worst nightmare come to pass.

The faces of the two boys flushed red with fear as the six sailors glared at them without a smile. Three of those men—if not all six—now knew who it was that had discovered them in the hold of the ship the day before.

"Ja, I bet they want to know...they do," said Aifke with a sinister-looking smile. "Maybe we can meet with them later and talk about it."

The boys gave a half-hearted smile. With a big gulp, Dillon managed, "Yeah, that sounds like a great idea."

With a sense of doom, both felt their fate was sealed.

Chapter 8
Ropes and Rumors

The USS *SkipJack* sailed nearer the coastline of New York every day, which meant that the Razor Pass problem would soon surface. The boys knew that they had to find out what was going on before it was too late. The Dutch-speaking sailors, knowing now who had overheard their conversations, were a constant concern of the boys. Their continued scowls of disapproval made the boys feel uneasy.

"We'll have to have a meeting," said Aifke one morning to Kyle, while he was on his watch. It sent chills up Kyle's back, and the boys tried to avoid Aifke at all costs. How long they could do so on a small ship was hard to tell.

In the meantime, Dillon and Kyle had to maintain their regular duties as well as keep up their training if they wanted to pass the test at the end of the program. On this particular day, the crew was practicing their entry through Razor Pass by tacking and maneuvering about ten miles out from the New Jersey coast. This way they would all be prepared when the time came.

"Bring her about!" Captain Blair ordered.

"Bring her about, Captain!" repeated Mr. Riggs. "Seventy degrees to the starboard, Bobby!" Mr. Riggs called out to Bobby, who was handling the wheel.

"Set the jibs to the breeze and raise the topgallant sail," Mr. Riggs ordered Ralph and Milk. Up the main beam they went, climbing high into the rigging so they could secure the sails to the yardarm.

Soon the trusty old ship began to cut her way through the waves. The captain continued to give one order after another, as if he were actually guiding the ship through the pass. First to the starboard and then to port, the ship tacked her way against the wind while at the same time moving forward.

"No wonder it's tricky getting the ship through the pass," Kyle commented as they pulled on the lines. One order after another had them working hand in hand with the crew. The lines lying on the deck began to tangle into coils.

"I'll hold this line while you straighten up the coils," Dillon said to Kyle.

"Okay," Kyle responded, dropping the line in his hand and kneeling to straighten up the lines on the deck.

The two were taught to keep their work area tidy and the lines free from knots. If they didn't, they could have a serious problem on their hands.

"Hey, look over there!" Dillon exclaimed to Kyle, pointing to the starboard side of the ship.

"Look at what?" Kyle asked, looking to see what was the matter.

"Look in the water. Dolphins!"

Trip of a Lifetime

"Wow, look at them glide through the water!" Kyle shouted as he leaned over the side of the ship.

Soon Dillon secured the line and joined Kyle, marvelling at the beautiful sight. "There must be a hundred of them!"

"Wouldn't it be fun to swim with them? It would be like sailing through the air."

"Hey, maybe we can do some fishing after

the training is over," suggested Dillon eagerly.

"That would be great!" Kyle chirped with delightful anticipation. "The last time we fished, I got me a big flounder that fed both of us!"

"Yeah, that was a whopper!" Dillon added. "Maybe this time I'll be the one to catch a big one."

"Yeah, maybe."

"To the halyard, main sail," came a command from the captain. Caught up in their conversation about the dolphins, the boys didn't hear the captain. "Dillon! Kyle! The mainsail! The mainsail!" sounded out the command from Captain Blair once again.

"The mainsail!" Dillon shouted with wide eyes and a blank stare at the sea.

"Oh, no!" Kyle added, swiftly turning on his heels.

As the boys hurried from the gunwale, they saw the glaring eyes of Captain Blair, Mr. Riggs and the other sailors.

Dillon ran to the pinrail to unloose the halyard, while Kyle tripped his way to his position. It took Kyle a little longer to get there, for he went down face first to the deck because of the tangled lines. Dillon, not seeing Kyle fall, turned from the pinrail and hurried to heave the lines and tripped over Kyle. The halyard slipped out of his hands, and the mainsail went flapping wildly in the wind.

The crew mates couldn't hold in their laughter at the unsightliness of Dillon and Kyle piled on top of each other and the lines tangled about their feet.

"Grab the lines and secure the sails!" bellowed Captain Blair with a scowl as big as Texas.

"All hands, steady to the wind. And a few of you go help with the mainsail!" fiercely commanded Mr. Riggs, realizing the seriousness of the situation.

In an instant the training was over, as the sailors rushed in to secure the mainsail and to correct the huge mistake the boys had made. Soon the ship was back in control and sailing smoothly.

"Dillon and Kyle, I want to see you down by

my cabin right away," the captain demanded as he stalked away with an unhappy disposition.

"Aye, aye, Sir," answered the boys as they slowly made their way to the cabin at the aft of the ship, their heads hanging low. They knew they had made a big mistake but didn't know what would happen next.

"Do you think we'll get kicked out of the program?" Kyle asked Dillon with a hopeless look.

"I don't know. If we don't get kicked out, we'll probably just get demoted and have to peel potatoes and clean the bathrooms for the rest of the trip."

They approached the cabin door and gave a knock. The captain stepped out to talk to them.

For the moment that the door was opened, the boys could see into the cabin of Captain Blair. They couldn't help noticing the many things hanging on the walls, evidence that he had been an experienced sailor for many years. There were pictures of him as a young man aboard previous ships and antique marine items that spoke of his love for the tall ships.

"Boys, I want to talk to you for a moment about a few things. First, what you did back there was a mistake that could have cost us the ship and our own lives had we been going through Razor Pass."

"We know, Sir. It was really dumb," spoke Dillon.

"'Dumb' is not the word, Dillon," continued the captain. "I think it is more like 'careless.' You lost your focus. It's easy for us to neglect our duties when exciting things happen, like those dolphins swimming alongside us today. Those wonderful things that God created are beautiful to behold, but there is a time to behold them and a time to do your duty."

"Yes, Sir," Kyle said meekly.

"I understand that you are still young and may not fully understand the importance of your roles on board ship, but everyone is counting on you. We all make mistakes. In fact, I recall doing something similar to what you boys did when I was an apprentice."

The boys lifted up their heads and looked at the captain in surprise. "You did?" said Dillon.

"Yes, I did, and I learned an important lesson that day, one I have not forgotten. If you boys will learn from this lesson and keep focused for the rest of the trip, I'll not send you home."

"Yes, Sir!" Kyle quickly replied.

"Yes, Sir! We learned our lesson, and we'll be the best boots on board for the rest of the trip!"

"I believe you will, boys," the kind captain continued. "If it were not for the fact that you have been doing such a good job and show-ing such enthusiasm in your duties, I might have to lay down a different punishment."

"Punishment?" said the boys in unison.

"Yes, I'm afraid I need to do something my captain did to me that day, which not only taught me a lesson but made it unpleas-ant as well. You see, you will be teaching the others that not performing your duty will result in some loss of privileges."

"Yes, Sir, we understand. You want us to peel potatoes or scrub the decks, don't you?"

"No, I have something else in mind. You will be cleaning the sails until we arrive, so

they will be ready for the race coming up."

The boys would rather have peeled potatoes. It was hard work cleaning those sails, work that normally only experienced sailors did.

"I'll have Mr. Riggs assign you right after lunch."

"Aye, aye, Sir," the boys said.

"And we want to apologize for what we did. Thank you for teaching us this important lesson," Kyle added. Of course he wasn't quite sure he meant it one hundred percent. It was like taking bitter medicine. You are thankful for the help but not for the taste.

"That's all. You're dismissed," said Captain Blair.

The boys left the cabin, relieved that they were not kicked out of the program. Every crew member, from the sailors to the boots, snickered and remarked to one another quietly as Kyle and Dillon returned to their post. The boys were extremely humiliated and disappointed in themselves.

"I don't think I like dolphins anymore," Kyle said in disgust.

"Me either. I hope I catch one the next time we fish," Dillon added with equal dislike. "I'm going to cook him in butter and enjoy every bite."

"Dillon! Kyle! Front and center!" shouted Mr. Riggs as he stood waiting amidships.

The boys hurriedly obeyed his order and stood at attention before him. "Yes, Sir," Dillon answered.

"The captain just informed me that you will have the privilege of cleaning the sails this afternoon and for the remainder of the week. I think he was too easy on you, but I've decided to put you with Aifke, Fritz and Hans."

Kyle gulped. "Did you say Aifke, Fritz and Hans?"

"That's right. Can't you hear, or do you need another trip to the captain's cabin to have your ears cleaned out?"

"No, Sir. No trip is necessary," Dillon quickly put in. "It's just that I don't think they like us," he continued uneasily.

"Sure they do. In fact, they came to me when they heard the good news and said they would like to take you under their wings personally and help you learn the fine art of scrubbing the sails," Mr. Riggs said insincerely. "They believe that with their guidance, the sails will never be cleaner."

"But...but..." Kyle stammered, trying to think of a way out of the dreaded chore.

"But nothing. Either you show up at six bells, or you'll be talking to the captain."

"Aye, aye, Sir," Dillon replied.

It was a long morning and an unenjoyable lunch as the boys anticipated the worst. They were fearful of what was in store for them with the likes of Aifke, Fritz and Hans.

★★★

Many things we do require our full attention. In fact, God says that we should give His Word, the Bible, our full attention. Read what it says in Proverbs 4:20–27:

"My son, attend to my words; incline thine ear unto my sayings.

"Let them not depart from thine eyes; keep them in the midst of thine heart.

"For they are life unto those that find them, and health to all their flesh.

"Keep thy heart with all diligence; for out of it are the issues of life.

"Put away from thee a froward mouth, and perverse lips put far from thee.

"Let thine eyes look right on, and let thine eyelids look straight before thee.

"Ponder the path of thy feet, and let all thy ways be established.

"Turn not to the right hand nor to the left: remove thy foot from evil."

Dillon and Kyle made the mistake of not paying attention to what they were doing. Christians can make the same mistake when it comes to living for God. Most of you reading this story are probably saved. You are good kids who love Jesus and want to do right. You obey when you are told to do something. However, you have probably said to your parents at one time or another, "I didn't mean to do it." The mistake you made was in not paying attention.

The boys let their guard down. They got their eyes on the dolphins. This was not a sin in itself, but their mistake was leaving their duty to watch them.

What are some areas where Christians need to give their full attention?

First, pay attention to Bible teaching. Solomon said in Proverbs 4:20, "My son, attend to my words; incline thine ear unto my sayings." In other words, Solomon was saying, "Pay attention to what I am saying." It is very important to pay attention to God's Word as it is read, preached or taught.

There are two ways to listen properly. We are told that we should "attend" and "incline." "Attend" in this passage means "to prick up the ears," and "incline" means "to spread out."

For twelve years I had a beautiful German shepherd dog. One of the things he would do if he saw a ground hog, cat or some other kind of animal was to stand perfectly still with his eyes focused on his prey. Then his ears would stand straight up, and the openings of his ears would spread out as he listened carefully to any noise he could hear. He was fun to watch as he put his shepherding skills into action.

Likewise, when horses hear something, their ears prick up and broaden. By turning their ears in different directions, they can hear more clearly. God designed horses in that manner so they can run from their enemies when they hear danger.

What I want to suggest to you today is that you give attention to the things of God. That doesn't mean you have to stop enjoying yourself. It simply means that while living your life and enjoying the things around you, you don't stop doing what's right.

Force yourself to give full attention to what is being said in church and Sunday school. That's not the time to write notes, talk, sleep or leave for the bathroom. Those things can be done at other times.

Second, pay attention to Bible salvation. This is important for obvious reasons. The Bible says, "For they [God's Words] are life unto those that find them, and health to all their flesh" (Proverbs 4:22).

When you give attention to those words teaching about salvation, it will help you understand the way to Heaven. Some kids fail to listen, so they don't understand how to be saved. Others may get distracted in church by kids' talking, passing notes or playing with toys. So listen to Bible preaching and teaching and learn how to be born again and how to receive eternal life.

Third, pay attention to Bible wisdom. Read again what it says in Proverbs, chapter 4:

"Keep thy heart with all diligence; for out of it are the issues of life.

"Put away from thee a froward mouth, and perverse lips put far from thee.

"Let thine eyes look right on, and let thine eyelids look straight before thee.

"Ponder the path of thy feet, and let all thy ways be established.

"Turn not to the right hand nor to the left: remove thy foot from evil."—Vss. 23-27.

To be wise means to be skillful in using God's Word. You are wise when you learn a Bible truth and correctly put it into practice. Dillon and Kyle knew about the workings of the topsails. They were not wise, however, when they failed to put that knowledge into action. Likewise, we can know what the Bible teaches, but if we don't put it into practice, we are not showing wisdom.

Proverbs 4, verses 23 to 27, gives us five wisdom facts that need to be observed:

#1—**"Keep thy heart with all diligence"** means we should carefully guard our heart and desires.

#2—**"Put away from thee a froward mouth"** means we need to watch what we say.

#3—**"Let thine eyes look right on"** means to keep our eyes on Jesus. Don't look at things that will lead you into sin.

#4—**"Ponder the path of thy feet"** means to think about the consequences of your actions before you do them. If something will lead to trouble, then avoid it.

#5—**"Turn not to the right hand nor to the left"** means don't get sidetracked along the way. If you see "dolphins," don't stop what you are doing to watch them. Stay focused on the task to which you are assigned.

These are some valuable lessons. Therefore, attend to wisdom, as Proverbs 5:1,2 tells us to do:

Trip of a Lifetime

"My son, attend unto my wisdom, and bow thine ear to my understanding:

"That thou mayest regard discretion, and that thy lips may keep knowledge."

Learn all the facts of wisdom. Learn carefully how to put them into practice. It is then that you will be what God wants you to be.

✬✬✬

"Hey, sailor boys!" sarcastically called Hans to Dillon and Kyle as they walked up the poop deck stairs.

"Well, look who's here," added Aifke as he gave Fritz a friendly push. "If it's not the sail cleaners."

"Ja, and lots of sails we have too," came the familiar voice of Fritz.

The boys now recognized the voices of the three men as the ones in the hold of the ship and in the store on Tangier Island.

"We should have lots to talk about, 'eh, boys?" Aifke asked.

The boys didn't say much as they walked toward the sailors.

"Reporting as ordered," Dillon said to Aifke.

"Good, because we are going to start right away!" he said sharply. "You will clean these sails right, or you might end up overboard."

"Overboard!" Kyle said, startled at such an idea.

"Ja, overboard with the dolphins you like so much," Hans said menacingly. "In fact, that is where you might end up anyway, if you don't keep your mouths shut!"

"Shut about what?" Dillon questioned.

"We both know about what. If you are smart, you will just lay low until this whole race thing is over," added Fritz.

"Ja, and besides, it's a big ocean—and accidents happen very easily," said Aifke ominously.

"If you're threatening us, we'll just go to Captain Blair!" warned Kyle with a meaning-ful glare.

"Ja, you do that. Go to Captain Blair and see if he listens to your rumors," continued Aifke.

"Ja, like he is going to believe a couple of troublemakers who can't even work the ropes."

"Ropes and rumors are all you have, and don't forget it," warned Hans.

The boys knew the sailors had a good point. There was no way Mr. Riggs or Captain Blair would listen to them after today's incident. Yet Dillon and Kyle knew they must do something before it was too late.

Chapter 9
The Daredevil Detective

The boys worked each night scrubbing the sails atop the forecastle, supervised by Hans, Fritz and Aifke. They worked the boys hard and intimidated them with threats. Dillon and Kyle knew they had to do something quickly because they would be at Razor Pass soon. Once there, who knew what might transpire.

One night while cleaning the sails, Dillon whispered to Kyle, "What are we going to do? If we don't get some proof soon, we might as well forget saving the *SkipJack*."

"I know. I overheard Aifke saying that he received the plans and hid them in his

footlocker," related Kyle.

"Really?" Dillon asked with interest.

"Yeah, I think if we can get those papers, we might have the proof we need to go to Captain Blair."

Dillon rubbed his head, thoughts racing through his mind. "But how can we get ahold of them? It seems as if there's always one of them lurking around, keeping an eye on us."

"I know. The only time they are all together is when we are cleaning the sails each night," added Kyle.

"Hey, what are you talking about?" growled Aifke.

"Oh, nothing," said Dillon.

"Well, you must be talking about something. If you're planning something, you'd better just forget it!" he added.

"Ja, we watching you carefully, we are," added Hans.

"It won't be too long before we get to Razor Pass. Then, we'll be allowed some shore leave," added Fritz.

"I don't think we want to go ashore," Kyle gulped.

"That's right. We're going to stay on board and get some things done," added Dillon. "Besides, we don't want to get lost in New York."

"Oh, don't worry about that," assured Fritz deviously.

"Ja, we already asked Mr. Riggs if we can take you ashore with us so we can make sure you are safe," chuckled Hans.

Aifke and Fritz laughed fiendishly. "That's right. We want to introduce you to some special friends of ours. They will be anxious to beat you—er, I mean, meet you," Aifke corrected, laughing even louder while the others joined in.

Dillon and Kyle couldn't share in their laughter.

The next day or two only made the boys more nervous and fearful. Yet each night they had to report to the forecastle and clean the sails. They wanted very much to tell Mr. Riggs or Captain Blair what was going on but doubted they would be believed. They must have proof.

Finally, one night they came up with a bold plan while cleaning the sails.

"Uh, Mr. Aifke, sir," stammered Dillon.

"Well, seaweed breath, what do you want?" said Aifke with a scowl.

"Well...ah...well...ah," he was so scared he could scarcely speak.

"Out with it!" Aifke demanded. "I've got better things to do than listen to you babble on!"

"What he wants to know is," Kyle stepped in, "if he can go to the galley. He isn't feeling very well, and he wants to get something for his stomach from Cookie."

"No, you can't," Aifke said harshly. "You can work sick for all I care."

With that, Dillon got a little bolder. "But I feel like I'm going to throw up," he said as he held his stomach with his right hand and his mouth with his left.

"The last time he got sick like this, it got all over the place," Kyle continued. "We'll have fish food all over these nice clean sails, and we have to have them done today."

"Well, all right, but be quick about it. And if you aren't back here in fifteen minutes, Fritz here will come looking for you!"

Slowly Dillon got up while looking at Kyle. "Be sure to keep them busy," he whispered. He began to walk toward the galley while the three watched him take his sickly looking steps in that direction. Once he stepped inside the galley, he had to go through the deckhouse and around the other side without being seen.

His heart was beating as he carefully rounded the corner of the deckhouse. There in plain sight were the three suspected criminals. Fortunately, Kyle could see Dillon's problem and let out a loud, "Ouch!"

The three men looked toward Kyle to see what had happened. "What's the matter?" asked Aifke.

"I got jabbed..." Kyle continued talking until he saw Dillon sneak into the quarters of the sailors. "I'm all right now," he told them.

Kyle's plan to divert the attention away from Dillon worked perfectly. The three sailors didn't suspect a thing and kept on talking with each other.

Dillon had to be careful as he made his way through the quarters. He was not allowed in there and had to make sure no one saw him. There was no way he could explain why he was in their quarters, and they might think he was stealing. That would only add to his dilemma with the captain.

Quietly he made his way to the bunk area, his heart pounding and sweat dripping off his forehead. *Now which one of these foot-lockers belongs to Aifke?* he thought to himself. *I remember his talking about it being fancy and coming from the Nether-lands.* He had begun to look for clues, when he noticed one of the crew mates asleep in his bunk. Then he saw the name Aifke writ-ten above the hammock right beside the sleeping crew mate.

"Great! Of all the bunks in here, his has to be right beside it," he grumbled.

I need to be quiet, he told himself. *Now to get to his footlocker.* Carefully and qui-etly, he made his way to the footlocker at the end of Aifke's bunk, praying that no one would come in and catch him or begin to look for him.

This looks like it, he thought. He knelt down in front of it and noticed something. *Oh, great! A padlock!* He put his sweaty hands on the small brass lock to see if it was locked. *Praise the Lord!* he happily shouted to himself. *It's open.*

Dillon cautiously slipped the lock from the hasp and laid it on the floor. Next, he pried open the top of the footlocker while trying to avoid any squeaking it might make. Then he leaned the lid against a beam by the bunk.

That paper has got to be in here some-where, he thought. Dillon rooted through the junk and set a bottle of cologne on the corner of the chest. *He must not know this is in here, 'cause he definitely doesn't smell that good.*

Still searching through clothes and other personal items, he came across a large army knife. It frightened Dillon a little, knowing that Aifke might not be afraid to use it.

What in the world? Dillon remarked to himself. A pink envelope with flowers on it

was not something he expected to find. Dillon couldn't help but feed his curiosity and read the return address. *Matilda!* he laughed. *He has a girlfriend named Matilda?* The back of the envelope contained a note "to my little dutchkins, Aifke-poo." It was too much for Dillon, so he put the letter back inside the chest. *I'll never look at him the same,* Dillon chuckled. Lifting a pair of pants and a shirt and setting them aside, he saw another envelope addressed to Aifke.

Hey, what's this? I bet this is what we're

looking for. He picked it up.

Dillon took a look around to be sure no one was watching and pulled out the letter. He examined this writing, which was partly in Dutch and partly in English. *I wonder what it says?* He flipped a page and noticed something else that caused him to know without a doubt this was what he was looking for.

Of course, we should not be going through things that belong to others. In this case, the men had as good as admitted they were doing something evil and likely destructive. Dillon and Kyle are seeking information that would lead to the discovery of the evil plot of Hans, Fritz and Aifke. The key to their success would be searching for the right things.

Christians likewise need to be seeking the Lord. Isaiah stated in chapter 55, verse 6, "Seek ye the LORD while he may be found, call ye upon him while he is near." Psalm 34:10 says, "The young lions do lack, and suffer hunger: but they that seek the LORD shall not want any good thing." David, the great king of Israel, found that when we seek after the things of God, we shall not want.

In a way, the Bible is like a Footlocker full of wondrous things for the believer in Christ. Those who have trusted Christ as their Saviour have some gifts that are made available to them by seeking for them. Just as Dillon carefully made his way into the bunk area to locate Aifke's footlocker and find the envelope, we are encouraged to find the Footlocker of God and locate His promises.

Let's open the Footlocker of God, the Bible, and peek inside. There are four things you will be sure to find and hopefully carry away.

The first item is peace. It says in Psalm 34:14, "Depart from evil, and do good; seek peace, and pursue it." This has the idea of getting along with people. In other words, find ways to get along with others. Pursue or run after this attitude and lifestyle. However, in doing so, depart from evil. If becoming a friend means doing something evil, then avoid that kind of peace and friendship. It is never right to do wrong, even trying to find peace.

Be the type of person that is described in Ephesians, chapter 4:

"Let all bitterness, and wrath, and anger, and clamour, and evil speaking, be put away from you, with all malice:

"And be ye kind one to another, tenderhearted, forgiving one another, even as God for Christ's sake hath forgiven you."— Vss. 31,32.

We have to understand that some will not be as kind as we would like them to be. Some people can be very unkind. Some folks are curt with their words and lack loving feelings. However, don't become like them; instead, show an attitude of kindness, be tenderhearted and quick to forgive.

If we look hard enough, we will find peace in God's Footlocker. Now reach inside; take it into your hand. Do you have it? Now place it in your heart and keep it there.

Let's see if we can find a treasure in Psalm 119. Open the lid and look in verse 45. **Sure enough, there is the second gift— the precepts of God:** "And I will walk at liberty: for I seek thy precepts."

King David said that he was seeking the precepts of God. A precept is a mandatory, or required, law written by God for all to follow.

What happens to those who live inside the precepts of God? The Bible says they have liberty. Liberty has the idea of walking in wide-open spaces.

Have you ever gone out into the country-side or to a state park? There you can do about anything you want—run or walk, sit or sleep, shout or whisper—as long as you stay within the rules of the park. There is a great joy in having liberty.

However, one who violates the rules of the state park, like setting trees on fire, will lose his liberty. He can be put in jail or fined. Oh, yes, he did as he pleased, but now he loses his freedom.

A person who sins against the precepts of God loses his freedom in Christ. He no longer lives in the wide-open promises and blessings of God but is hampered and closed in by the problems sin brings.

Why not open the lid of God's Footlocker, look inside the envelope of precepts and remove the liberty that you have in Christ?

The third gift we are taught to seek

for is good. Read what it says in the Book of Amos, chapter 5, verses 14 and 15:

"Seek good, and not evil, that ye may live: and so the LORD, the God of hosts, shall be with you, as ye have spoken.

"Hate the evil, and love the good, and establish judgment in the gate: it may be that the LORD God of hosts will be gracious unto the remnant of Joseph."

What is "good"? It is that which is positive and desirable in quality. It is the opposite of evil. The word "evil" came from the idea of spoiled food. Evil is something to be despised and cast away, not to be fixed for dinner. The Devil has made evil appear to be desirable, but God considers it rotten food. Therefore, seek out good rather than evil, just as these verses instruct you to do. Certainly, good is a worthy item to be sought for in God's Footlocker.

The last quality we need to seek is meekness. Zephaniah 2:3 commands:

"Seek ye the LORD, all ye meek of the earth, which have wrought his judgment; seek righteousness, seek meekness: it may be ye shall be hid in the day of the LORD's anger."

Meekness has the idea of being humble rather than being proud. Being proud is when one takes credit for something he has done, not recognizing that God, and perhaps other people, made it possible. A humble person, on the other hand, realizes that he is a product of God and God's use of others in his life, that he has become what he is because of the influence, investments and hard work of God and man.

A proud person will not call on God for help, and rarely will he seek the help of others. He feels he doesn't need anyone's help; he is self-made and independent.

It is important to note that Jesus was meek in His approach to life. In chapter 2 of Philippians, verses 8 and 9, we are told that the mind of Christ caused Him not to treat mankind with an attitude of prideful arrogance even though He was God. Jesus humbly submitted Himself to death on the cross to meet the needs of His creation.

Search out meekness in the Footlocker of God, and you will find it.

What Dillon found was a hand-drawn map

marking the location of Razor Pass and Governors Island, though they had misspelled it "Govenor's Island". *This is it!* he almost shouted out loud. *If I can get this to Captain Blair, it might be the proof we need. Just hold on a little longer, Kyle.*

He took the letter and map, folded them neatly and stuffed them in his pocket. He found a piece of paper lying on the floor and placed it inside the envelope to make it appear that nothing was missing. Carefully he laid the envelope back inside the foot-locker. Then he replaced the shirt, pants and other items. Slowly he lowered the lid of the footlocker, trying to keep it from squeaking or slamming shut.

"Ding-ding, ding-ding, ding-ding, ding-ding," sounded the bells.

Dillon just about jumped out of his skin, and let out a hushed, "Aggh."

He saw the sailor sit up and look around. In a sleepy daze he looked right at Dillon. "Aye, aye, Mr. Riggs," he said. Then the man just plopped back into the bunk and returned to snoring as before.

Whew, that was close! Dillon thought. He finished closing the trunk, replaced the padlock and crept along the floor. Then he made his way out of the sleeping quarters, up the stairs and to the doorway.

"Now, I need to get out of here without their seeing me. I hope Kyle can come up with another diversion tactic."

Dillon popped his head through the doorway, and it appeared that Kyle had timed it just right. Aifke and Hans were apparently asking him something. They had him pinned against the forecastle mast and seemed to be giving him a tough time. It was the perfect chance to slip out and walk around the deck-house without being seen.

"*One, two, three,*" he counted silently. Then, keeping his eyes on them, he darted to the left and around the corner of the deckhouse away from their view. Whew! He'd made it. He felt like a superhero! He was Dillon, the daredevil detective. He was all things mysterious. He was all things courageous. He was—

Dillon ran right into Fritz's chest as he rounded the corner. He froze in fear.

"So, what are you doing!" came the firm voice of Fritz, who was standing with his arms crossed and glaring at Dillon with a menacing scowl.

"Nothing," he replied fearfully. "I got lost and was just coming back, that's all." Dillon, the daredevil detective, must have taken a back door, because suddenly he felt nothing like courageous.

"No, you are up to something, you are!" Fritz growled, grabbing him by the arm and whisking him toward the others. "Here he is," he said to Aifke, "and he wasn't in the galley. He was in our bunkhouse."

Fritz pushed him toward Aifke, who was none too happy about it. "So, what were you doing in the bunkhouse?" he demanded.

"The bunkhouse? What bunkhouse?" Dillon tried to look innocent.

"You know what bunkhouse. The only bunkhouse on board ship," Hans asserted forcefully. "And what is that sticking out of your pocket?"

"That's a letter from home," he answered, covering it with his hand.

"Well, let's have a look at it," Hans said, snatching the folded pages from his pocket. Dillon protested, but to no avail, as Hans opened them up. "Hey, this boot has the letter and map from Captain Heimler!"

Suddenly Dillon realized that he had been repeatedly lying just to get out of trouble, and it had done him no good at all. They would have to trust God to preserve them, as they should have all along.

Chapter 10
The Three Musketeers

"Well, aren't you glad you ran into Fritz?" Aifke said with a sinister smile. "Just think what would have happened if the captain had got ahold of this."

"Ja, he might have put us peeling potatoes for a week," snickered Hans.

"That would have made us upset. It would have ruined our friendship," Fritz added laughingly.

Aifke folded the letter and map and walked to the gunwale railing and dangled them over the side of the ship. "Oops, clumsy me," he said, letting them drop to the water below.

Dillon and Kyle didn't know what would happen next, but they weren't going to wait to find out. Cookie, who was just coming out of the galley, was the perfect person to run to.

"Hey, Cookie, what's for supper?" they asked, turning around to see what the thugs were doing. The three just stood there watching from the forecastle without seeming to worry.

The boys knew they had had a close call, but they also knew they had lost their evidence. The letter and map were gone. Now they would have to take their chances that something would turn up closer to race day.

For the rest of the day Aifke, Hans and Fritz ignored the boys. Dillon and Kyle couldn't decide whether this was good or bad.

The *SkipJack* maneuvered safely through Razor Pass and slowly traveled her way into the New York Harbor. They anchored just offshore, near one of New York's most historic landmarks, Governors Island. It lies about a half mile off the tip of Manhattan and was for many years a military post for the U.S. First Army. The island, a tourist sight, was the meeting place for the upcoming tall ship race.

Dillon and Kyle had the first part of the anchor watch that evening from eight o'clock to eleven o'clock and were enjoying the warm summer breeze with Dillon even steering awhile. The lighthouse could be seen off their starboard, and the moon began to shine through the clouds, leaving its reflection on the calm harbor waters.

"How are we going to get out of going ashore?" asked Kyle that night. "We'll be taken hostage by Aifke, Hans and Fritz."

"I don't know," Dillon answered. "We'd better stay low and try to get out of going ashore. Our only chance is to ask Captain Blair if we can stay on board and learn something from Mr. Drake."

"What are we going to learn? We've already learned everything my brain can stand."

"Don't worry. He'll think of something. I'm sure there is something that will keep us from being kidnapped by the likes of Aifke, Hans and Fritz's friends. Our secret sleuthing mission, Operation Tangier, has to be kept alive, and so do we!"

"You're right. We'd better find the captain right away," Kyle said.

The next morning Dillon and Kyle managed to convince the captain they needed to stay aboard as planned, much to the dismay of Aifke, Hans and Fritz.

Along with their crew mates, the three saboteurs went ashore, but they were going to formulate their evil deed. The two boy sleuths had no idea what lay ahead, and their detective work seemed to be heading nowhere. Their main concern was the safety of the *SkipJack* and the crew.

Dillon and Kyle walked to the forecastle and made their way onto a large boom, or mast, called the bowsprit. It projected from the very front of the ship and carried sail in order to govern the fore part of the ship and to counteract the force of the aftersails at the stern.

The bowsprit jutted out from the front of the ship, which allowed the boys to hang over the water below. Of course, there was a safety net so they couldn't fall to the water below and get hurt. It was a good place to talk privately and to figure out what they would do next.

"What are we going to do?" Kyle questioned as he watched the sea gulls swirling around the ship.

"I don't know, but if we don't figure out something, we may be joining those fish down there," Dillon answered, pointing to the water.

"Hey, Dillon! Look there!" Kyle pointed to the anchor chain that was holding the anchor of the ship in place.

"What's that?" Dillon asked, as he noticed something white sticking to the top of the chain near the hawsepipe.

"That looks like the letter Aifke threw overboard!" Kyle exclaimed. "It must have blown back on the anchor chain and got stuck there!"

"Let's get it!" said Dillon, hurriedly making his way to the side of the ship. "One of us needs to climb down there. I'll hold a rope while you make your way down."

"What do you mean, *you'll* hold the rope? Why do *I* need to do it?"

"Okay, I'll go down. Just hold the rope secure, and make sure you don't let go," Dillon relented, fearlessly.

"Maybe we ought to throw a rope ladder over the side. There's one up by the bowsprit. It will be safer and easier than trying to pull on a rope."

"Good idea!" Dillon agreed.

He quickly ran over to the ladder and brought it to the side of the ship. The boys secured it and then lowered it into position. Carefully Dillon climbed over the side of the ship, while Kyle observed from above.

"Are you all right?" Kyle asked, concerned for his safety.

"Yes, I'm fine, just a little further...a little further...a little more...I got it!"

With the letter safely tucked in his pocket, he made his way up the ladder and back on board. After returning the rope ladder to its place by the bowsprit, the boys quickly ran to their cabin and unfolded the papers.

Sure enough, the letter and the map were in good condition, except for a portion of the letter that had been torn as the anchor was lowered the day before. Although some of it was missing, they would still have been able to make out what was written in the letter, except for one thing.

"This is written in Dutch!" Kyle said.

"Great! How are we going to read it?" Dillon grabbed the paper from Kyle's hands in frustration and scrutinized the map. "The only thing we can tell for sure is this is where they will make their move."

"But what are they going to do?" Kyle wondered. "It looks like there is a rocky, dangerous area where the arrows are pointing."

Along with the X on the map were small shapes of ships. One ship had the letters DT beside it, while the other was labeled SJ. Kyle looked at the spot marked with a red X and raised one of his eyebrows in confusion.

"Do you think SJ stands for *SkipJack?*" Dillon questioned.

"I bet it does, but what does DT stand for?" Kyle kicked at the floorboard in impatience.

"That is the next question that needs to be answered," Dillon answered.

The boys had to figure out some way to decipher the letter. They couldn't take it to the three Dutch thugs, so who else could interpret the letter? It had to be one of the other Dutch sailors on the *SkipJack*, but whom could they trust?

As evening came, the whaleboats, full of laughing crew mates, made their way back to the *SkipJack*. Dillon and Kyle were saddened that they had not gone ashore with them, but at least they were safe and confident in their success. They knew they would have to be careful in which person they confided. Even though Aifke, Hans and Fritz worked together, that did not mean the other Dutch sailors weren't in on the plot against the ship.

"We've got to bring up a conversation with them somehow and probe them for information," Dillon schemed with Kyle.

"I agree. But we have to be careful what we say, or we could end up where we were yesterday."

"Which of the three other Dutch sailors do you think we can trust?" Dillon asked.

"What about Joord? He seems nice."

"Nice? Are you kidding! He never says 'hi.' And look at his eyes. They're narrow and beady. My cousin Danny says never trust anyone with narrow, beady eyes. No, not Joord. He'd turn us in for sure."

"How about Epke? He seems trustworthy," Kyle tried again.

"Well, maybe, but I've seen him talking to Aifke many times. I'm not sure about him either. Did you ever look at his black hair? My cousin also says that black hair means you have a dark past."

"Well, the only one left is Koenraad," declared Kyle.

"I don't know...did you see his lower lip?" Dillon hesitated.

"What about his lower lip?"

"Well, my cousin says that the lower lip is the picture of the soul. The lower the lip, the lower the person's honesty," answered Dillon, with full assurance of the reliability of his source.

"That's ridiculous!" Kyle laughed. "There is no way you can tell anything by someone's lower lip, their hair color or the narrowness of their eyes."

"Everyone is entitled to their opinion." Dillon lifted his chin, annoyed by Kyle's doubt. "Besides, you haven't given a good reason why we *should* pick him."

"Well, his name means 'bold counsel.' A person's name means something, you know."

"That's true," Dillon conceded. "But if he is a crook, then his name doesn't matter."

"I remember talking to him a few weeks ago, and he seemed friendly and honest enough. In fact, he told me that he writes to his mother every week and goes to church when he is home."

"Really?" Dillon asked, optimistically.

"That's right. He has a sense of humor too, and the captain said he was one of the best sailors he had. If we get him on our side, then maybe the captain will listen to us. I think he's our man."

"Me too," Dillon affirmed. "Except we still have to put him to the test. Tomorrow we'll talk to him and see what happens."

"Agreed!" Kyle said, slapping Dillon's hand in a high-five.

Did you ever take a look at the size of the anchors used by large ships to prevent or restrict their movement? The anchors, which bury their broad, hooklike arms on the sea floor, are huge. Therefore, the chains need to be large enough to hold the ship to the anchor without breaking.

A ship floating unanchored could easily drift into dangerous situations. It might land upon rocks, get beached on the shore or drift far away from its destination. The anchor gives assurance to the crew that the ship is safely secured.

An anchor is a picture of hopeful security.

The stronger the anchor, the more hope there is that the crew will be safe. Paul uses an anchor to illustrate eternal life in Heaven. Read Hebrews 6:13–19 with me and see what I mean:

"For when God made promise to Abraham, because he could swear by no greater, he sware by himself,

"Saying, Surely blessing I will bless thee, and multiplying I will multiply thee.

"And so, after he had patiently endured, he obtained the promise.

"For men verily swear by the greater: and an oath for confirmation is to them an end of all strife.

"Wherein God, willing more abundantly to shew unto the heirs of promise the immutability of his counsel, confirmed it by an oath:

"That by two immutable things, in which it was impossible for God to lie, we might have a strong consolation, who have fled for refuge to lay hold upon the hope set before us:

"Which hope we have as an anchor of the soul, both sure and stedfast, and which

entereth into that within the veil."

Think of your life as a ship anchored safely in a harbor. When you trust Jesus as your Saviour, the anchor of salvation connects you to Heaven. The anchor and chain are permanent, unbreakable and reliable. Once saved, you will never have to doubt it. Our future hope of eternal life is assured, and Paul uses this example of an anchor to show us that.

Let's take a look at our heavenly anchor and consider two important truths.

First, the anchor pictures God's Word. Dillon and Kyle were not sure they could trust Koenraad. However, when it comes to God's Word, we know it is trustworthy, for God cannot lie.

In Titus, chapter 1, verse 2, God says, "In hope of eternal life, which God, that cannot lie, promised before the world began." In other words, God cannot lie.

So when God told us in Romans, chapter 10, verse 13: "For whosoever shall call upon the name of the Lord shall be saved," we know it is true. When we call on God to save us, after realizing Jesus is the Saviour, He saves us. He said He would, and since He cannot lie, that verse is an anchor lodged in Heaven with a chain attached to our hearts.

God's Word is unchanging and, therefore, reliable. Once God says something, it is permanent. He won't tell us later on that He changed His mind about our eternal life.

Even when we doubt God, Timothy tells us that He is faithful to His Word: "If we believe not, yet he abideth faithful: he cannot deny himself" (II Timothy 2:13). If God were to lie, then He would be a sinner just like us.

Second, the anchor is God's promise. Just like His Word does not change, neither do His promises. God uses Abraham as an example of His unchanging promises. Although Abraham lied two times, God still kept His promise. Let's look at this story in Genesis 22:16,17:

"*By myself have I sworn, saith the* LORD, *for because thou hast done this thing, and hast not withheld thy son, thine only son:*

"*That in blessing I will bless thee, and in*

multiplying I will mulitply thy seed as the stars of the heaven, and as the sand which is upon the sea shore; and thy seed shall possess the gate of his enemies."

Because of Abraham's faith in trusting God to deliver Isaac, God promised to bless him. Since that day to now, God has kept His promise. It has not changed. That promise was made through an oath, or covenant.

Sometimes in today's world, if we want to purchase something, we must sign a contract, or a written covenant, showing our intentions to pay for it. With salvation, God signed our contract of eternal life with the blood of Jesus Christ on Calvary. It was sealed with His resurrection.

God's promise of eternal life is not affected by man's lifestyle or mistakes. Eternal life is based upon a promise made by God. Remember, once God says something, He is bound by it. He absolutely cannot lie! Therefore, even if you aren't perfect, God still honors His contract.

Jesus' blood has been shed for you. The resurrection of Jesus verified it. You can completely trust the anchor of your soul. It will not slip, it will not be unloosed, and the chain will not break.

Have you trusted Jesus as your Saviour? If you have, then you can be assured that God will keep His promise. If you haven't, why not do it right now? Bow your head and ask Jesus to be your Saviour and then yield your life to Him from this day forward.

Only one day was left before the race. Dillon and Kyle knew they had to act on their plan that day, or it would be too late. The letter was their only chance, and it seemed that Koenraad was their last hope.

They approached Koenraad as he was storing the block and tackle below the poop deck.

"Hey, Koenraad, do you need some help?" Kyle offered eagerly.

"Isn't this your time off?" he responded.

"Yes, it is, but we're kinda getting bored and wouldn't mind helping you."

"And besides, we'd like to ask you a question, if you don't mind," Dillon added, not willing to waste any more time.

"Ja, why not. Just grab that tackle and bring it over here," Koenraad instructed, happy to have the help. "You know, boots, I've always liked you two, and I think you're doing a great job despite what happened the other day."

"Thanks, Koenraad, we like you too," Kyle said, smiling.

"Now what is it that you wanted to ask me?" Koenraad inquired.

Kyle looked over at Dillon and nodded his head, as if to say, "Go ahead and tell him."

"Well, Koenraad, can you keep a secret? I mean a BIG secret?" Dillon stressed seriously.

"Sure, as long as it isn't illegal," he said, laughing.

"Well, no, it's not illegal—at least not our part of it," Dillon continued.

Koenraad got serious and stopped what he was doing. "What do you boys mean?"

"We found a letter," Kyle went on, looking around to be sure no one was listening, "and it has a map and some Dutch writing on it."

"It doesn't sound illegal to me," Koenraad said, probing for more information. "Do you have the letter and map?"

"Well…" Dillon hesitated while scanning the area for anyone that might be listening.

"Go ahead; you can trust me. I'll not tell a soul," he assured them.

"Go ahead, Dillon; give him the letter," Kyle prodded.

Dillon slowly reached to his pocket and pulled out the letter. "We believe someone is trying to sabotage the *SkipJack* in the race tomorrow."

"Sabotage the *SkipJack*," Koenraad repeated in disbelief. "Are you sure?"

"Yes, Sir, we are. In fact, they even told us they were and that we needed to keep our mouths shut if we knew what was good for us."

"Who? And why didn't you tell Captain Blair?" he questioned.

The two explained the whole matter to Koenraad, not leaving out any detail. They told him of Tangier Island, the letter, the map, Razor Pass and the meeting the day before on Governors Island.

Koenraad read the letter from Captain Heimler and told them that it detailed the plans to run the *SkipJack* into the hidden rock barrier during the final leg of the race. There was money in it for Aifke, Hans and Fritz, if they were successful.

"I would never have believed they would do such a thing! This is certainly good proof, boys. I can't doubt you for one minute with this letter. And the map plainly points out the *SkipJack* and the other ship marked DT."

"We saw that, but we weren't sure what it meant," Kyle probed.

"The letters stand for *Dutch Treasure*. That's the ship from the Netherlands, and Captain Heimler is her captain."

"I knew it!" Dillon exclaimed. "We've got them for sure now!"

"Maybe. There is one problem, boys." Koenraad said this with concern.

"What's that, Koenraad?" Dillon asked.

"It's only a letter. Unless we catch them

red-handed, they could deny that they were actually going to do it. Besides, Captain Blair can't read Dutch. It would be our word against theirs."

"What can we do?" Kyle asked, his hope deflating as quickly as a life raft with a hole in it.

"We will wait until the race begins tomorrow. Then, when they prepare the lines to cause the accident, I'll go with you to the captain and reveal the entire plot. He may not believe you, but he should believe me when he sees them in action."

"That's what we were hoping. Thanks, Koenraad. We'll do what you say," said Dillon.

"You put this letter in your pocket and don't let anyone find it. Then, when the race begins, meet me in the bathroom with the letter. It's then that we'll go to Captain Blair and catch them red-handed."

"We'll be like the three musketeers!" Kyle said excitedly. "'One for all, and all for one.'"

"That's right," Koenraad said, putting his hand out. The boys reached in to stack their hands on top of his, and they all repeated, "'One for all, and all for one.'"

Chapter 11
The Silver Anchor

Three-masted tall ships were anchored snugly at the starting line of the race. Ships' colors were hoisted from the main masts of the various ships while spectators watched with anticipation from Governors Island. Excitement could be felt in the air as the crews waited for the firing of the gun that would begin the race. Once the gun went off, the crews would hoist their anchors and head for the finish line. Whatever crew could perform the best and cross the finish line first would be the champions for that year.

Dillon and Kyle stood proudly, but they

were still a bit fearful for what lay ahead. Hopefully, they would be able to uncover the deeds of Aifke, Hans and Fritz before the hidden rocks tore open the *SkipJack*'s hull, leaving her to sink to the bottom of the harbor. They prayed together that morning that the USS *SkipJack* would sail in front and pull off a victory.

"What do you think is going to happen, Kyle?" Dillon asked quietly.

"I'm not sure, but I know one thing. Whatever happens, we are going down fighting!" he emphasized with a fist in the air.

"I believe if Koenraad can pull off this plan, we will have nothing to worry about," Dillon continued.

"You're right, Dillon. We're fortunate to have Koenraad working with us. With his help, we ought to catch those three thugs without a problem."

"I know. I can't wait to see the look on their faces when they are caught red-handed," Dillon chuckled.

"That will be awesome," Kyle added. "They deserve everything they will get."

"Attention, all captains!" Dillon and Kyle could hear the announcement from a loudspeaker just offshore of the starting line. "The race will begin in five minutes. Prepare all hands."

Captain Blair stood proudly atop the poop deck and spoke a few brief words. "Fellow sailors, this is your big day—a day to prove to yourselves and to the world that we have the best crew and the best ship afloat."

Cheers came from the crew as they heard the challenging words. The sun was shining above the horizon, the sky was partly cloudy, and the breeze on the waters made it a perfect day for sailing. Every sailor stood ready for the command—or almost every man. Dillon, Kyle and Koenraad knew that three of their crew had evil intentions for the *Skipjack* and hopes for the ship *Dutch Treasure* to win.

"Every man ready at the post, and be prepared to weigh anchor at my command!" he shouted so every sailor could hear. Captain Blair stood at attention, listening for the sound of the starting gun.

"Ready!" echoed the warning slowly, followed by a pause.

"Set!"

"BANG!"

In a flash, men began to scurry up the rope ladders to unloose the sails; others dashed for the jib sails. "Anchor's aweigh!" shouted Charles, a fellow recruit. Orders from the captain and mates were sounding out, and each member of the crew jumped to his command as quickly and efficiently as possible.

The *SkipJack* began to pull out in front, with the *Dutch Treasure* close beside her. Other ships were in pursuit, but the *SkipJack* plowed ahead. Dillon and Kyle weren't to meet Koenraad until they made their approach to Razor Pass. It would be then that they would reveal the plot of the three treasonous sailors.

The ships' crews fought hard to take the lead, but in each turn of the course the *SkipJack* would maneuver to keep the lead. The *Dutch Treasure* was always close to taking the lead and kept to the starboard of the *SkipJack*.

Finally, the ships were approaching the turn

which would lead them through Razor Pass.

"It's time to go, Kyle," said Dillon. "We've got to meet Koenraad in the bathroom."

"Do you think he's there?"

"Yes, I saw him walking in that direction; let's go!" commanded Dillon.

They boys left their positions and made their way to the bathroom area. It was dark inside, so Kyle ventured a whisper, "Koenraad, are you in here?"

"Ja, just step inside and turn the light on."

When Kyle flipped the switch, the boys jumped in surprise. Aifke, Hans and Fritz grabbed them and held their arms behind their backs.

"Hey, what are you doing?" yelped Dillon as he tried to wrench himself free.

However, the answer didn't come from Aifke or Hans or even Fritz. It came from Koenraad, who was standing behind the boys with some rope and tape in his hands. "We are meeting as planned," Koenraad said laughing. He enjoyed watching their faces drop as they realized they had been tricked.

"You know what, boys? This time you went too far," said Aifke. "I tried to warn you what would happen if you kept up with your detective work. Come with us!"

Only a few minutes passed before tape covered their mouths and rope tied their hands and feet.

"Put an Out of Order sign on the bath-room door," Koenraad commanded Fritz. The three locked the door from the outside, and the boys could hear them talking. Dillon and Kyle could do nothing but look at each other with horrified expressions. What would their captors do now?

"We have only one choice," said Aifke. "We must throw them overboard!"

"How are we going to do that? We are sure to get caught."

"It's easy," Aifke assured them. "All we have to do is wait until the *SkipJack* runs into the hidden rocks. During all the commo-tion, we can take them topside and throw them overboard. We will tell the others that one of them fell overboard and the other one dove in to rescue him."

"Do you think it will work?" questioned Fritz, wrinkling his forehead in uncertainty.

"Sure. By the time the ship turns around, they will be long gone! They'll be shark bait!" assured Koenraad with a sinister smile. "Hans and Fritz can watch the door; we'll go back to our posts. Once the ship hits the rocks, we'll come back here and get rid of them."

The boys heard every word and could read each other's mind. They had to get those ropes loose and get out of there. But could they do it? And how would they escape?

Keep trying to loosen the ropes, thought Kyle as he tried forcing his hands one way, then the next.

The ropes were just too tight for them to do anything. The time was slipping away. Dillon looked at Kyle, his eyes asking, *What are we going to do?*

Kyle bowed his head and began to pray. Dillon followed his lead and began to pray as well. They remembered the promise that God would see them through it all, that He had angels watching over them and that they were "born again." Knowing Jesus was their

Saviour brought peace to their hearts.

Kyle looked up and rolled over to Dillon. He then positioned his mouth by Dillon's hands so that Dillon could pull the tape away from his mouth. Dillon, understanding what Kyle was doing, grabbed the corner of the tape with his fingers. Kyle pulled away, releasing the tape from his mouth. Dillon repeated the maneuver to get the tape from his mouth. At least now they could talk.

"What if we just yell for help?" whispered Kyle.

"No. They will come in here and knock us out. I've got a better idea."

"What's that?" Kyle asked, his heart pounding.

"Remember that sliding panel that Milk used to sneak into the galley?"

"Hey, that's right!" Kyle caught on and brightened up. "If we can open it, maybe we can get out of here!"

Both quietly inched their way over to the secret panel. Dillon leaned against it and began to push with his back. "It won't budge!" he said.

"Try using your feet," Kyle urged.

Dillon swung around and put his feet against the panel. "It's moving a little. See if you can help."

Kyle made his attempt, and the panel began to slide. As soon as it opened, the boys worked their way into the dark galley and then closed the panel.

"Man, it's dark in here!" Kyle remarked.

"It sure is. But if we can work our way over to the knives, we can cut ourselves loose."

As they did, they could hear a commotion in the bathroom. "Hey, they're gone!" shouted Hans to Fritz. "Go get the others!"

"Where did they go?" asked Fritz frantically after he had returned with Aifke and Koenraad.

"The panel door," shouted Aifke. "Remember, that panel slides open!"

"Hurry, Kyle, hurry!" Dillon prodded.

The panel door began to slide open, and Hans' head popped through. "There they are!" he called to the others.

Kids, hold tight, and I'll tell you what happened next, right after the Bible lesson.

★★★

Dillon and Kyle were making a difficult choice in standing up to the likes of Aifke, Fritz and Hans. Likewise, the apostle Paul had to take a stand against Emperor Nero in the first century. In II Timothy 4:1,5-8, Paul said:

"I charge thee therefore before God, and the Lord Jesus Christ, who shall judge the quick and the dead at his appearing and his kingdom."

"Watch thou in all things, endure afflictions, do the work of an evangelist, make full proof of thy ministry.

"For I am now ready to be offered, and the time of my departure is at hand.

"I have fought a good fight, I have finished my course, I have kept the faith:

"Henceforth there is laid up for me a crown of righteousness, which the Lord, the righteous judge, shall give me at that day: and not to me only, but unto all them also that love his appearing."

To defy Nero meant death for the apostle Paul. Nero had already put many Christians to death, and Paul would be a trophy.

Paul, nearing the end of his life and in prison for preaching the Gospel, said, "I am now ready to be offered, and the time of my departure is at hand." He was talking about being martyred, or put to death.

Why would Paul be willing to die for his faith? He believed that one day he would stand before God to give an account of his life, so he wanted to finish the job God had given him and be faithful to his Lord.

In our story, Dillon and Kyle tried hard to be brave sailors. They knew the risks involved but believed they must do what was necessary. As Christians, we must sometimes make difficult decisions when it comes to living for God. There will be times when we are tempted to take the easy path, which may not be the right thing to do.

We must realize, as Paul did, that we will have to stand before God and explain why we did the things we did. We want Him to be proud of us, don't we? We want Jesus to smile and reward us for a job well done.

So how do we prepare for that day? Paul, our example, has the answers.

First, he chose the right course. He said in verse 7, "I have finished my course." Paul used the illustration of running a race to show what our work for God is like. We can even compare it to the ship race in our story. The most important thing for us is to get in the race. God expects that of us.

It may be hard to know what the right way is, especially since you are so young.

Maybe your race is to be a good witness. Show your brothers and sisters how much you love Jesus. Show your friends how much Jesus means to you so they will want to get saved too.

Your race might be preparing for the future by doing the best you can in school. It might be doing a good job at home, obeying your parents and having a good attitude. But make a decision now that you will find ways to serve God.

Second, Paul "kept the faith." It is not easy to stay in a race. It takes work to continue in anything, especially living for the Lord. That is because we have three enemies—the world, the flesh and the Devil.

Paul also had human enemies to face. Maybe he was tempted to stop serving God to avoid the difficulties, but he didn't because he loved the Lord Jesus with all of his heart. He owed Him many thanks for his eternal life.

Dillon and Kyle loved the captain, the *SkipJack* and her crew. They were grateful for what they had learned and received. Now they weren't about to quit.

Are you thankful toward God? Those blessings and gifts from God will give you reason to keep your faith in God and in His Word.

Third, Paul believed the promise of one day being rewarded for being faithful. One day we will stand before the Lord. Jesus will give out rewards to all those who were faithful, to those who didn't quit and to those who gave out the gospel message.

One day you will meet Jesus face-to-face. Will you be rewarded? You will not be rewarded for how smart you are, what grades you got in school or how many clothes you owned. You are promised a reward for how you served God.

Dillon and Kyle were hoping to graduate as honorary sailors at the end of their trip. They wanted Captain Blair to say to them, "Well done!" Likewise, Paul wanted the Captain of his salvation, Jesus, to say, "Well done!"

I trust that is your desire as well. I trust that you will always keep in mind that you have a God who loves you and wants you to be successful in your life serving Him and man.

"We don't have time for a knife," shouted Kyle. "Knock over the pots and pans! Make noise!"

The boys began to shout for help and knock over anything that would make noise. Hans began to work his way through the panel door. Fortunately, it was rather small, and he was having difficulty squeezing through. Pots and pans began falling and clanging on the floor, but with the race going on, it was doubtful anyone could hear.

As Hans made his way through, he caught up with Kyle, put his hand to the boy's mouth and picked up a pan. "Be quiet, or I'll knock you over the head!" he ordered.

The boys stopped and lay there looking at Hans in the darkness, with Fritz, Koenraad and Aifke peeking through the hole.

"Drag them back in here," ordered Aifke.

All of a sudden a light came on, and there stood Cookie, pointing a shotgun at Hans. "You'll not drag them anywhere!" he said sharply. "You men get your hands up!"

Cookie untied the boys and sent Kyle to get help. Soon the captain stood in the doorway, wanting to find out what was going on. Dillon and Kyle explained the plot and handed him the map showing the location of the hidden rocks.

"Koenraad switched Mr. Norman's navigational maps so he wouldn't know about the hidden rocks," Dillon said excitedly. "We are headed for them as we speak."

The captain quickly walked out of the galley and shouted to Mr. Riggs, "Hoist the top sails and take down the jib sails. Hard to starboard!"

The sailors obeyed the commands. Soon the *SkipJack* was slowing down and turning away from the rocks. "Hard to port. Drop the jibs and top sails," he commanded. Once again the wind hit the sails, and the ship turned toward the finish line.

The ship avoided the danger of the rocks, but as it did so, the *Dutch Treasure* pulled ahead and crossed the finish line. The *SkipJack* came in a close second, and the race was over. The crew wondered why the captain had given orders that caused the *SkipJack* to lose the race.

After the *SkipJack* was anchored in the harbor, Captain Blair allowed Dillon and Kyle to explain the whole story to the crew. They told of their suspicions on Tangier Island and how it led to the discovery of the letter and map in Aifke's footlocker.

Before the night was out, the four criminals were boarded on a harbor police boat on their way to jail, and the boys were resting quietly in their bunks.

"You know, Dillon, I believe God was watching over us," Kyle said.

"You're right," Dillon agreed. "Our guardian angels must have been working overtime." They both laughed and were soon fast asleep, happy that it was finally over.

The next morning, Captain Heimler of the

Dutch Treasure joined Aifke, Hans, Fritz and Koenraad in jail. Disqualified for cheating, the *Dutch Treasure* was forced to forfeit the race.

The *SkipJack* was now the rightful winner of the race. Before a crowd of spectators and crew members of the various ships, the trophy was presented to Captain Blair. It was a proud moment for every man and boy on board.

That afternoon as the crew of the USS *SkipJack* was standing at attention amidships, the captain proudly handed out the honorary sailor patches to every one of the recruits. They were also given official sailor uniforms and hats to show everyone that they were no longer recruits but real sailors aboard the best tall ship on the high seas.

Finally, Dillon and Kyle were called to stand before the captain, Mr. Riggs, Mr. Jars and Mr. Norman.

"Dillon, Kyle, we want to thank you for your heroism in saving the USS *SkipJack* and her crew from certain destruction," Captain Blair announced. "Never in the history of the *SkipJack* have two boots

achieved such dis-
tinction. It is my
honor to award you
with our highest
award, the Silver
Anchor, in recogni-
tion of your brav-
ery in saving the
SkipJack and her
crew. This award
has been given out
only four times in
the history of the
SkipJack's days at
sea: once to the first captain over sixty
years ago for valor during World War II,
once to myself when I was a first mate, once
to Mr. Riggs and Mr. Norman for their heroism in saving the *SkipJack* during a bad
storm, and now today to both of you."

Dillon and Kyle grinned from ear to ear as
Captain Blair proudly pinned the medals to
their uniforms. They stepped back and salut-
ed the officers while the crew threw their
hats in the air and let out a loud cheer, "Hip,
hip, hooray! Hip, hip, hooray! Hip, hip, hooray!"

Dillon and Kyle looked at each other in

triumph. They knew that this was a summer well spent, a true adventure, a trip of a lifetime.

THE END

Appendix Contents

⚓ Dutch Words & Translation

⚓ Glossary of Sailing Terms

⚓ Sailor Knots

⚓ Vertical Masts Details

⚓ USS SkipJack Decks

⚓ Ship's Sail Names

⚓ Ship's Rigging

⚓ Installing a Mast

⚓ Weighing Anchor

Dutch Words and Translation

Chapter 5

"We zullen elkaar by de vergader plaats ontmoeten. Als we bij Razor Pass zijn kunnen we ons plan uitvoeren." =

"We will meet you at the meeting place. When we get to Razor Pass, we can put our plan into action."

Chapter 6

Moeten = have to

Dat = that

Dit = this

Plan= plan

Taak = parts

Noit = never

Ja = Yes

All-lain-maar = all we want

Zein = meet up

Day teye uhs = details

Glossary of Sailing Terms

Aft—toward the rear of the ship.

Aloft—above the deck of the ship.

Amidships—midway between the bow and the stern. Also called, midship.

Aweigh—the position of an anchor as it is raised clear of the bottom.

Bell, or *Bells*—the system used to keep time aboard ship. The ship's bell, near the steering wheel, is rung each half hour with a characteristic number of strokes. Midnight is eight bells, 12:30 is one bell, 1:00 is two bells and so on until 4 A.M. when 8 bells are sounded. Then the process begins all over.

Binnacle—a structure near the steering wheel that houses the compass.

Block—a pulley on which line or cable turns.

Bosun, or *Bo'sun*—a junior officer aboard a ship whose responsibility is to maintain the deck of the ship and rigging. The term came from the word boatswain, or boat lover.

Trip of a Lifetime

Bow—the forward end of the ship.

Bowsprit—the wooden pole projecting forward from the front of a ship from which sails are set and masts are supported.

Buoy—an anchored float used for marking a position on the water.

Cabin—an enclosed compartment in a ship; used as shelter or living quarters.

Chart—a map for use by navigators.

Coil—to lay a line down in circular turns.

Course—the direction in which a boat is steered.

Crow's-nest—a platform for the lookout on a mast.

Deckhouse—a low building constructed on the top deck of a ship.

Dinghy—a small, open boat used to transport passengers to and from a larger vessel.

Dog watch—either one of two two-hour watches between 4 P.M. and 8 P.M.

Fathom—a depth of six feet.

Fish—to bring an anchor to the rail and secure it.

Forecastle, or *Fo'c'sle*—the crew's quarters which could be a deckhouse behind the foremast.

Forecastle Head—a short deck in the front of a ship raised above the main deck. The jibs and anchors are handled from here.

Forward, or *fore*—toward the bow, or front of the ship.

Gig—a small boat carried by a ship and used in port by the captain when going ashore. Also called a dinghy.

Going about—a term referring to the process of tacking a ship.

Gunwale—the top edge or railing of a ship to prevent sailors from falling overboard.

Halfdeck—the living quarters for apprentices.

Halyard, or *halliard (Haul Yard)*—the tackle used to hoist sails, or yards.

Hawsepipe—a small opening in the bow of the ship through which the anchor chain passes.

Heave to—to stop a ship's forward motion by turning into the wind.

Jib—a triangular sail.

Knot—one nautical mile per hour. A nautical mile is equal to 6,080 feet.

Lay to—to go.

Lead Line—a line with a lead weight attached to determine the depth of the ocean bottom under a ship.

Lee, or *Leeward*—the word "lee" means to be covered or sheltered. It is the side of the ship sheltered from the wind.

Lighthouse—a structure that shelters and displays the navigational lights of the ship.

Mast—wooden poles used to secure the sails, or yards. In the first ships there was one mast pole, called the "main mast." As ships were made larger, another pole was attached above the main mast called the "topmast." Above the topmasts were the "topgallant masts." Still another mast was attached called the "topgallant mast royal." There could also be a total of four main masts in the largest ships. From bow to stern they are the bowsprit, foremast, main mast, and mizzen mast. *See: Sail chart #'s 1,2,3, and 4.*

Mizzen—the third mast on a ship.

Mudhook—another term for an anchor.

Navigation—the art and science of conducting a boat safely from one point to another.

Navigation Rules—the rules governing the

movement of vessels in relation to each other.

Poop deck—the raised deck in the aft portion (rear) of the ship.

Port—the left-hand side of a ship. So named because this was the side ships were loaded from when in port.

Ratlines—foot rests for seamen ascending or descending the rigging.

Rigging, Running—all the moveable wires, rope, cordage, chains and blocks by which the sails are set and controlled.

Rigging, Standing—all the fixed wires and chains by which the masts are secured and braced.

Shrouds—part of the standing rigging. Heavy wires secured to the ship's hull and to the mast tops to provide lateral support.

Spanker—the lowest fore-and-aft sail on the after mast, a short fourth mast of a ship. (see: sail names chart, #34)

Starboard—when facing forward, the right-hand side of a ship.

Stern—the rear of the ship.

Tackle—pulleys and line used for creating power when hauling sails, boats and anchors. (See: "Ship's Rigging" section of appendix)

Topgallant mast—the mast above the top-mast. (See: "Sail and Mast Names" chart)

Topmast—the mast above the main mast. (See: "Sail and Mast Names" chart)

Topsides—the sides of a vessel between the waterline and the deck. Sometimes refers to onto or above the deck.

Under way—Ship in motion when not at port or anchored.

Windlass—a type of winch adapted for hauling in anchor cable. In the *SkipJack*, the windlass was man powered by way of a vertical, spool-shaped cylinder called a cap-stan.

Windward—going the opposite direction the wind is blowing.

Yard—a long pole, tapered at the ends to support the top of sails. They attach to the masts at their middle.

Yaw—to swing or steer off course.

Yardarm—the end of a yard.

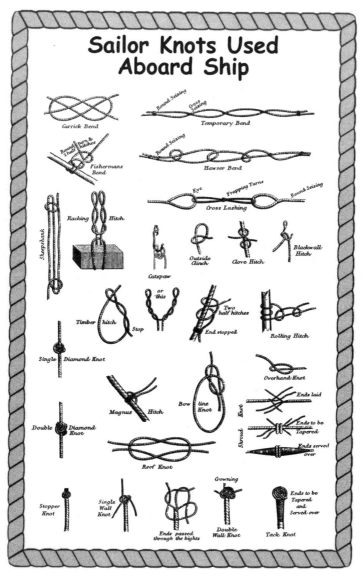

Sailor Knots Used Aboard Ship

Carrick Bend

Round Seizing · Cross Seizing
Temporary Bend

Round & 2 half hitches
Fishermans Bend

Round Seizing
Hawser Bend

Sheepshank

Racking Hitch

Eye · Frapping Turns · Round Seizing
Cross Lashing

Catspaw

Outside Clinch

Clove Hitch

Blackwall Hitch

Timber hitch · or this · Stop

Two half hitches · End stopped

Rolling Hitch

Single Diamond Knot

Magnus Hitch

Bow line Knot

Overhand Knot

Ends laid

Shroud Knot

Ends to be Tapered

Double Diamond Knot

Reef Knot

Ends served over

Stopper Knot

Single Wall Knot

Ends passed through the bights

Crowning
Double Wall Knot

Ends to be Tapered and Served over
Tack Knot

Vertical Masts

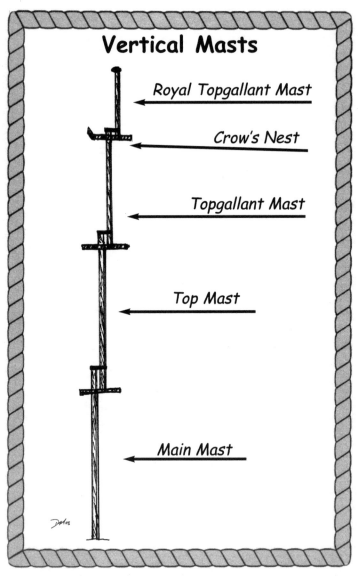

Royal Topgallant Mast

Crow's Nest

Topgallant Mast

Top Mast

Main Mast

Sail Names

1. Foremast
2. Main Mast
3. Mizzen Mast
4. Bowsprit
5. Flying Jib
6. Outer Jib
7. Inner Jib
8. Fore Course
9. Fore Topsail
10. Fore Topgallant Sail
11. Fore Royal Sail
12. Main Royal Staysail
13. Main Topgallant Staysail
14. Main Topmast Staysail
15. Main Course
16. Main Topsail
17. Main Topgallant Sail
18. Main Royal Sail
19. Mizzen Royal Staysail
20. Mizzen Topgallant Staysail
21. Main Spencer
22. Mizzen Topmast Staysail
23. Crossjack, Mizzen Course
24. Mizzen Topsail
25. Mizzen Topgallant Sail
26. Mizzen Royal Sail
27. Spanker

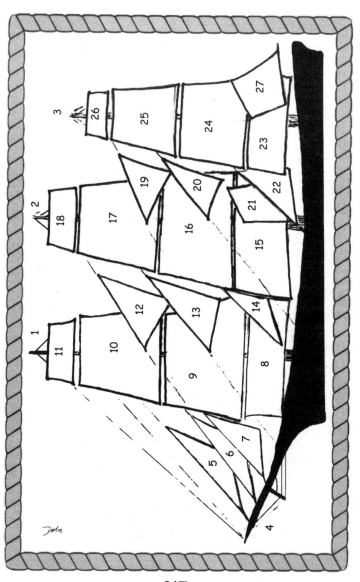

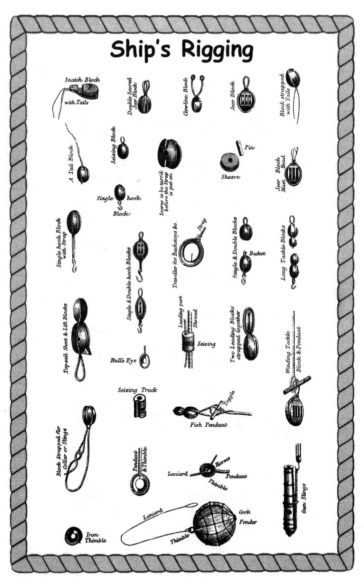

Ship's Rigging

Installing a Mast

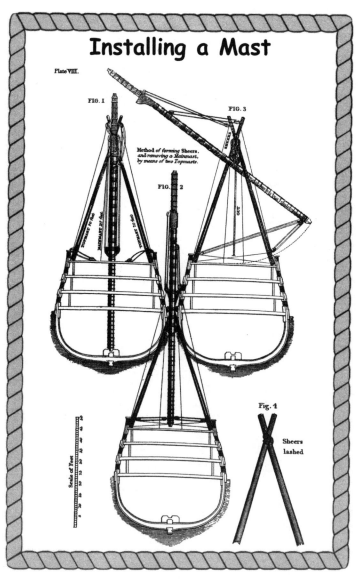

Plate VIII.

FIG. 1 FIG. 3

Method of forming Sheers, and removing a Mainmast, by means of two Topmasts.

FIG. 2

Fig. 4

Sheers lashed

Scale of Feet

Weighing Anchor With a Capstan

In some of the old tall ships, the anchors were brought in with the use of a capstan and windlass. As the men turned the capstan, the chain came through the "hawsepipe," an opening in the side of the ship for the purpose of channeling the chain into the ship. The chain rounded the windlass and worked its way into the hold of the ship for storage.

Men were stationed in the hold in order to neatly coil the chain, or rope in some ships.

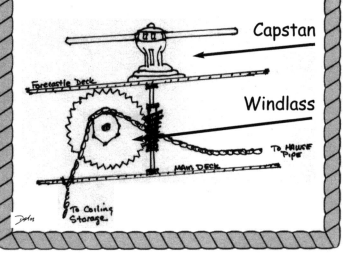

Capstan

Windlass

Forecastle Deck

To Hawse Pipe

Main Deck

To Coiling Storage

For a complete list of books available from the Sword of the Lord, write to Sword of the Lord Publishers, P. O. Box 1099, Murfreesboro, Tennessee 37133.

(800) 251-4100
(615) 893-6700
FAX (615) 848-6943